CHASING BIGFOOT

Art Coulson

BRAINERD'S BATTLE OF THE BOOKS
SPONSORED BY: ISD #181, BPSF &
FRIENDS OF THE PUBLIC LIBRARY

REYCRAFT
B O O K S

Reycraft Books
55 Fifth Avenue
New York, NY 10003

Reycraftbooks.com

Reycraft Books is a trade imprint and trademark of Newmark Learning, LLC.

Text © 2022 Art Coulson
Illustration © 2022 Reycraft Books

Design elements: Ajwad Creative/Getty Images; Andrius_Saz/Shutterstock; iulias/Shutterstock; Krasovski Dmitri/Shutterstock; PeterPencil/Getty Images; Tartila/Shutterstock; Thanee Hengpattanapong/EyeEm/Getty Images

Photo of Judaculla Rock: Luanne Allgood/Shutterstock
Author photo: Courtesy of Art Coulson
Illustrator photo: Courtesy of Frank Buffalo Hyde

Library of Congress Control Number: 2021921193
ISBN: 978-1-4788-7547-5

Printed in Dongguan, China. 8557/1121/18421
10 9 8 7 6 5 4 3 2 1

First Edition Paperback published by Reycraft Books 2022.

For my father, the original Art Coulson

Contents

Page

Prologue Tsul'kalu Has a Vision 1

1 Where Am I? 6

2 The Journey Begins 10

3 A Tsul'kalu Story 18

4 The Fix Is In 24

5 The Journey Ends—for Now 28

6 The Rock 37

7 Treasure Hunters Join Forces 44

8 The Little Person 50

9 Treasure Hunters Plan 58

10 The Rock Speaks 66

11 I Spy with My Little Eye 74

12 Uktena and His Crystal 76

13 Chooch Opens Janees's Eyes 81

14 They're After Me! 86

15 Finding Bigfoot 92

16 Time to Regroup 94

17 The Messenger 97

18 Janees Walks into a Trap 102

19 Will Anyone Believe Us? 109

20 The Mothman 116

21 Predators 120

22 Home of the Mothman 122

23 Stealthy Stalkers 127

24 Plan B—or Is It C? 130

25 Kidnapped 135

26 Back to Their Lair 137

27 Where's Chooch? 139

28 Janees Comes Clean 143

29 Dr. Almasty's Daydream 147

30 Back at the Hideout 149

31 In Hot Pursuit 154

32 Coming To 159

33 The Treasure Map 163

34 A Little Help 167

35 Another Task 172

36 The Omen 174

37 The Chase Is On 181

38 The Fourth Option 188

39 The Battle 191

40 The Message 198

41 Saying Goodbye 204

PROLOGUE

TSUL'KALU HAS A VISION

Tsul'kalu

Tanasee Bald, sometime in the not-too-distant past, nighttime

"The Boy is coming," Tsul'kalu said to the Little People crowded around him in his cave. The giant, covered in dark hair, was seated on a carved stone chair. Still, he towered over the Little People by several feet.

The light from the fire danced around the uneven walls like dancers at a stomp dance. The fire gave Tsul'kalu's slanted eyes a red glow. The cave was silent, except for the occasional sound of a drip in its dark recesses or a random pop and crackle from the fire.

"How do you know he's coming now?" asked one of the Little People, a man about three feet tall with a dark brown face and long black hair wrapped in a bright blue turban. "We've heard the stories, but they don't tell us when he will be coming to carry our message out to the world."

Tsul'kalu looked at the Little People, moving his gaze from face to face. Then he used his massive hairy arms to push his body up and out of his seat. The Little People looked up at him.

"I saw him in a dream," Tsul'kalu said, placing a large hand gently on the blue-turbaned man's shoulder. "He is a Cherokee boy, as the stories foretold. He is coming from far away, traveling with his family. He doesn't know his part in this story, but he soon will. And when the time is right, he will be able to understand our message and become our messenger."

All the Little People began to talk at once, excitedly discussing the Boy's imminent arrival. They spoke an ancient form of the Cherokee language, the version still spoken by animals and spirit beings. Modern-day Cherokee people might not be able to speak it, but they would be able to understand the meaning.

Tsul'kalu held up his hand and the cave again grew quiet.

"But there's something I need you to do, Awatisgi," he said to the blue-turbaned man. "It's very important."

Awatisgi stood up a bit straighter and looked up into Tsul'kalu's eyes. "Anything, Tsul'kalu. You know we are ready to do our part."

"Osda. Good, good," the giant said as he turned to walk to a part of the cavern outside the fire's glow. "I have something for you."

All the Little People watched with rapt attention.

Tsul'kalu stepped back into the light and held a leather-wrapped bundle out in the palm of his hand, cradling the bundle with his seven fingers.

"Take this to the place I showed you before and give it to the Boy. He will be there Wednesday morning," Tsul'kalu told Awatisgi, handing the bundle to the Little Person. "Show him how to use this, but caution him about its power."

Awatisgi unwrapped the corners of the bundle and peeked inside. He took a step back, as if that would put some distance between him and the item he still held in his small hand. The other Little People gasped and started to talk loudly again.

"Yes, it's what you think it is, ginali," Tsul'kalu said in a calming voice. "But it is what the Boy needs if he is to see the world as we see it. He will not understand the message until he can do that."

Awatisgi folded the bundle carefully and tucked it into the beaded bandolier bag he wore across his shoulder.

"Gado usdi? What is it?" asked a woman dressed

in a red-and-blue tear dress as she tugged at Awatisgi's sleeve.

Awatisgi looked quickly to Tsul'kalu, who responded with a slight shake of his head.

"I can't say for now," Awatisgi replied. "But one day, when the old men tell this story about me, you will get your answer."

Tsul'kalu put his hand on Awatisgi's shoulder again and looked him in the eyes.

"What I'm asking you to do is dangerous," Tsul'kalu said. "There are people and forces lined up against us who do not want our message out in the world—people who care more about riches than they do the world itself. I ask you, Awatisgi, because I know you can do this and you won't let us down."

"Hawa," Awatisgi said. "I will do what needs to be done. And I will do so without fear or hesitation."

With that, Awatisgi turned and walked toward the cave entrance.

As the Little Person reached the opening, an owl called out. Its mournful song reverberated around the cave.

Awatisgi staggered a moment, as if he had missed his step. The temperature in the cave seemed to drop several degrees.

Awatisgi straightened and looked back at Tsul'kalu and the Little People. He shivered, but then shook himself off and continued his journey.

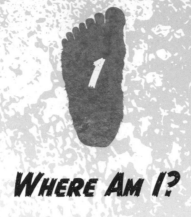

WHERE AM I?

Chooch Tenkiller

In a dank cellar somewhere,
Saturday? Sunday?

My head hurts, I can't see, and I can't feel my hands. What a way to wake up.

But I'm not in my bed or slumped in the back seat of our car.

Where the heck am I?

Too dark to see. But everything seems wet and drippy. Stinky.

I smell something nasty, like our basement in Minneapolis. Kind of like dirt, wet cardboard, and old leaves. Mom would probably say, "Chooch Tenkiller, that smells just like the inside of your lacrosse bag." But she says that about every foul odor she smells. She is a one-note drum, as Grandma would say. I don't know what that means exactly, but I guess you get the idea.

Now, where was I?

Oh, yeah. It's not just dark—there's something over my head. I'm tied up in some place that smells like an old cellar. And I have a thumping headache and a sharp pain in my neck.

How could I forget?

I hear muffled voices from somewhere far away. Above me? Loud thumps. Something being dragged.

Then I hear a door close. Was that the sound of chairs sliding across a floor? The muffled voices grow clearer. I can make out some words and parts of sentences. The voices are scratchy, as if the people talking need to clear their throats.

"...the Boy. We have to..."

Are they talking about me? What am I doing here? I can't remember how I got here.

Am I still in West Virginia? That's where we stopped on our way home. My uncles wanted to tour some museum dedicated to a monster called a Mothman. I'm not making that part up. My uncles are really weird. They just have to stop at every monster museum and roadside attraction when we're on a road trip.

Did I mention my head really hurts? I don't feel like I'm thinking clearly.

"…the treasure. He can read the rock…"

What rock?

These guys aren't making any sense. You don't read a rock. That's crazy talk.

"Afterward, we'll just have to get rid of the kid. He's no good to us…liability…"

A chill works its way up my spine and tingles at the back of my neck. I shiver and that makes my head hurt even more.

But that last bit of tough talk helps my mind start to clear. My memories come flooding back in from the darkness.

The road trip to the mountains of North Carolina.

My uncles telling stories at some conference.

My cousin Janees.

Our visit to a Cherokee sacred site called Judaculla Rock to check out its cool markings.

My encounter with the Cherokee Little People.

A magic crystal…

Seeing Bigfoot?

Really? Bigfoot?

Maybe those last three are scrambled memories caused by whatever knocked me out, combined with my uncles' stories. I'm not really sure.

But one thing I do know: I have to figure a way out of here and find my uncles and my cousin.

And to think this all started with a fart joke.

THE JOURNEY BEGINS

Chooch Tenkiller

On the road, the Monday before

"I've heard fart jokes before. I'm not easily embarrassed."

My cousin flopped down into the back seat of the car, flipped her long black hair, and rolled her eyes at me. Miss Drama. As if to emphasize her point, she put her right hand up under her purple Oglala Lakota Powwow T-shirt and made a farting noise under her left arm. How mature. Hard to believe she was going on thirteen.

I jumped a little when my uncle Jack slammed the back hatch and walked toward the driver's door. He slapped the top of the car four times before he slid in—

for luck—then worked his belly around the steering wheel and poked the key in the ignition. He started the car and twirled the radio dial until he found a country station. My uncle Dynamite smiled and started to sing along to a song about some guy who was apparently lonesome and calling his cattle. Basically a nonsense song. With yodeling, no less. I. Kid. You. Not.

"It's not the jokes you have to worry about," I said, turning to glare at Janees.

I mean, come on. My prissy cousin was about to be stuck in a smelly old car with two elders and a teenage boy for two whole days.

There would be venison sausage. Cheese. Flatulence. It could get ugly. Even I was a little scared. And I'm fearless. More or less. We were on our way from our home in Minneapolis to North Carolina, where my uncles would tell stories at some plant research thing at Western Carolina University. I can't remember what they call it. It's where a lot of people sit around at a college talking about stuff and acting really smart. I asked Janees if she knew what the talking thing was called, but she just shrugged her shoulders and straightened her sweatshirt. Anyway, whatever they're called, we go to them quite often because my family is full of storytellers. Professional ones—they actually get paid to tell all the old Cherokee stories I get to hear for free. Over and over again.

I really don't like to go on these trips, but I don't have much choice. Mom tells me these trips with my uncles are "part of my education." Not education like going to school and solving math problems. She means another kind of education, one that sends chills up my spine every time she mentions it: the dreaded cultural education. That's where I learn more about being an American Indian and how I'm supposed to act in all sorts of situations. I fought this battle long ago and lost. I mean, really, why should a kid have to continue his education in the summer or on weekends when his friends are all riding their bikes or playing sports? It's like I get punished for being an Indian or something.

But wait, we were talking about something far more interesting than my sad life.

Farts.

"Just keep your gas to yourself, Chooch, and pass me one of those comics," Janees said, settling back into the cold vinyl seat. She pushed the hair out of her face and reached out a hand for a book.

"I'm telling you—this is your last chance to escape." I handed her the first issue of *Locke & Key*. "I've been on these storytelling trips before. There's nothing to do. And you'll be doing it with a bunch of guys. You should stay home with your mom and my mom. You could have some uninterrupted mom and auntie time."

"I already got enough 'mom time' on the trip to your house, locked in a car for nine hours with my mom singing Disney songs at the top of her lungs—all the way from Porcupine to Minneapolis."

We'd made that trip to Porcupine, aka Nowhere, South Dakota, a few times to visit Janees and her family, my aunt Brandy and my uncle Zack, on the Pine Ridge Reservation. Uncle Zack was Lakota. He met Aunt Brandy at Haskell Indian Nations University in Kansas. A lot of Indian people from all different tribes go to Haskell. Even Jim Thorpe, the great American Indian athlete, went there.

I know what it's like to be cooped up in a car with your parents and other assorted relatives for long periods of time. Except in our car, we didn't have any Disney tunes. We had only two kinds of music, as Uncle Dynamite liked to point out: country and western. You know, the kind of songs where some guy whines and howls about his missing cows or some lady screeches about her cheating boyfriend. Sheesh. Remind me never to date a cowgirl. On second thought, remind me never to date.

Oh, yeah, and I should probably mention here that Dynamite isn't my uncle's real name. But you probably already guessed that. His name is Harold. But no one ever calls him that. You see, his snoring is legendary. Some nights after supper, he falls asleep in his chair and the dynamite starts going off. Or at least that's what it sounds like. A lot of Indian people have nicknames like that. I mean, come on, you don't think my given name is Chooch, do you? I'll tell you a little secret. My real name is Maurice, but no one—I mean no one—calls me that.

Uncle Dynamite folded himself into the front passenger seat and slapped his brother, my uncle Jack, on the shoulder. "Let's hit the road, Jack."

He laughed himself silly.

Yeah, that joke never got old. For him. I mean, that old song, "Hit the Road, Jack," was popular when my grandma was a girl. I knew it only because Uncle Dynamite insisted on playing it before every road trip with Uncle Jack.

"Off to tell some lies, right, Dynamite?" Uncle Jack replied with a chuckle.

I have to explain a little bit here. Uncle Jack was making a joke because the Cherokee word for telling a story—gagoga—means "he's telling a lie." Pretty funny, huh? We Cherokee people can be real comedians. I'd learned that much in my cultural education "classes" on the road.

"Yes, indeed, brother," Uncle Dynamite said. "But what I'm really looking forward to is getting a glimpse of an asduleni."

"Quite right, brother, quite right," Uncle Jack said. "We've been looking for Bigfoot a long time. This will be our best shot at finally seeing him alive and in person."

"Asduleni?" I said. "I don't know that word."

"It's the Cherokee word for Bigfoot," Uncle Jack said. "Well, one of them anyway. While we're in North Carolina, we'll be visiting one of our sacred sites—they call it Judaculla Rock. It's where Tsul'kalu left his mark. Some people say that Tsul'kalu was one of the ones they call Bigfoot. But we don't know for sure."

He got that faraway look in his eyes that could mean only one thing—a story was coming on.

"Buckle in," I told Janees. "It's about to get deep in here."

Janees looked up from *Locke & Key* and raised an eyebrow.

"What?" she said.

"Uncle Jack is about to unleash one of his stories on us," I told her. "This is how it is every road trip. Uncle Jack and Uncle Dynamite swap stories the whole way. It's hard to get any sleep or listen to the radio. It's what I was warning you about. That and the flatulence."

"Whatever," Janees said, turning her attention back to her comic book.

"This is what the old men told me when I was a boy. Tsul'kalu is a spirit being," Uncle Jack started.

"Notice he said 'is,'" interjected Uncle Dynamite. "Never trust a storyteller who speaks of a spirit being in the past tense."

"Ahem. As I was saying," Uncle Jack said, tossing a quick glare at his brother. "Tsul'kalu is a spirit being. He's bigger than a man—some say he is a giant. He has long hair all over his body and his eyes are slanted. That's how he got his name—Tsul'kalu means 'he has them slanted.' The eyes part was just understood, you know."

I nodded. Sometimes I have to nod, or say, "Mmm hmm," to make my uncles believe I'm paying attention. Which I was, sort of.

"Tsul'kalu lives up on a hill called Tanasee Bald, there in western North Carolina, near where we're going to tell stories," Uncle Jack said. "The old people say he marked a rock up above Cullowhee that they call Judaculla Rock. The yonega—the white people—call it Judaculla in English because they couldn't pronounce his Cherokee name right. They do that a lot. Anyway, they say Tsul'kalu jumped down from his house to the hilltop where the rock is to get a drink from the creek there and left his prints on the rock. They know they're his prints because he has seven fingers on each hand

and seven toes on each foot. They say he also made markings in the rock that no one can read."

"Mmm hmm," I said.

See what I did there?

"Your uncle Dynamite and I want to see the rock for ourselves—see if we can read it," Uncle Jack said. "Plus, maybe we'll get to see Tsul'kalu. Some stories about him say he is one of the asduleni. A Bigfoot. We've been looking for Bigfoots all our lives. This could be our chance to find one."

"Well, go on, tell us the story, brother," Uncle Dynamite said. He turned back to look at Janees and me and winked.

A Tsul'kalu Story

Janees Hollow Horn

Somewhere south of Minneapolis, a few moments later

"Ilvhiyu tsigesv, in the forever that was—a long time ago—Tsul'kalu made his mark on a rock high on a hill below his home," said my uncle Jack.

I settled back in my seat and peered at my uncle over the top of my comic book.

"Tsul'kalu, like I said, is a spirit being. The old people say he is a giant, covered in long, dark hair. This is why so many people think he is related to the Bigfoots everybody is seeing all the time," Uncle Jack said. "Especially back home in Oklahoma. They say Tsul'kalu came with us on the Trail of Tears."

I glanced over at Chooch and made a funny face, but he didn't crack a smile. Chooch frowned at me and gave his head a quick shake, then turned back to look at my uncle. Chooch actually seemed interested. I turned back to my uncle and put on my own "interested" face as he continued his story about this Joolgaloo fellow.

"Tsul'kalu watches over all the game animals, the ones we hunt," Uncle Jack continued. "He is their protector. He makes sure that we have enough to eat. He also makes sure no one takes too many animals or shows any of his creatures disrespect.

"That's one reason we have to know the proper words to say after we've had a successful hunt. We must show the animals our respect. We must thank them for giving us their meat so we can feed our families.

"Tsul'kalu watches over the animals from his home up on Tanasee Bald, the cleared-off top of a mountain where he sat in what they call his Judgment Seat. He cleared the top of the mountain a long time ago and it's still cleared today, up there where the Tuckasegee River starts. He called it 'the place where everything was white.'"

"Are we going there—to the Tennessee Bald place?" I asked. Chooch shot me a look.

"Shh," he said softly. "We're not supposed to interrupt a story."

"No, Wesa," Uncle Jack said. He called me by my nickname, which is Cherokee for "cat." It's an uncle thing. "We won't be going up there this trip."

I shot Chooch a look of my own, one that said, "Mind your own business—I can ask a serious question if I want to."

"As I was saying," Uncle Jack continued. "One time, a group of hunters came to Tsul'kalu's lands. Some say the hunters weren't Cherokee, but from another tribe nearby. Others say they were Cherokee people who had forgotten our ways. That part isn't important.

"The hunters climbed Tanasee Bald that day. And as they climbed the mountain, the hunters killed rabbits and squirrels and deer and bears. They killed so many that they couldn't begin to carry all the animals. They just cut off the best parts and took trophies. The hunters left the animals where they had fallen. The men did not stop to say the right words. They did not apologize to the animals for taking their lives. They did not thank the animals for feeding their families. They didn't even leave a gift of tobacco. They just killed and laughed and kept climbing Tsul'kalu's hill.

"Tsul'kalu saw what they were doing. He grew angry. He reared back and roared. They say his roar echoed through those hills like thunder. He was raising a powerful storm, and those hunters didn't see it coming until it was too late.

"Tsul'kalu stepped down from his Judgment Seat and began to run down the mountain. Trees shook and fell as he passed. The very ground quaked with each step he took.

"The hunters heard what they thought was thunder and stopped near the top of the mountain. They looked for a place to take cover in case of a storm. Then, one of the hunters gave a terrified shout. He pointed up the mountain at the giant, Tsul'kalu, who was running at them.

"The hunters dropped their bows and blowguns and fled. They cried and wailed as they ran down the mountain.

"They got to the big rock and stopped to catch their breath. They had lost Tsul'kalu. Or so they thought.

"The giant gave a big roar and leapt off the hillside above them, landing on the big boulder they call Judaculla Rock today. Where he landed, he left a handprint. As I told you, we know it's his handprint because it has seven fingers, just like Tsul'kalu's does.

"The hunters screamed and began to run down the hillside, running along the river toward the valley below.

"Tsul'kalu called a warning after them. He told the hunters never to return. He also told them to keep our ways—to respect the animals we hunt. To ask for their permission and forgiveness when we take one to feed our families. He told them not to hunt for fun or sport. He told them not to take trophies.

"Those hunters never came back. Tsul'kalu returned to his home. And as he walked up his mountain, he touched each of the fallen animals. They each in turn got up and ran off, alive and whole again.

"He had returned balance to his world. And he still maintains that balance today.

"You know why that's important, right?"

Chooch and I looked at Uncle Jack and nodded.

"If we hunt too much or kill all the fish, we won't have anything to eat in the future," Chooch said.

"The Lakota have the same belief," I said, sharing a bit about my father's tribe. "Not the Bigfoot part. The part about respecting nature and keeping things balanced."

Then I shook my head and sighed. "Okay, I lied— we also have our own Bigfoot stories. My auntie Fawn saw one on Highway 18 south of Wounded Knee last year."

Chooch laughed.

"What's so funny?" I asked.

"Nothing," Chooch said. "I was just picturing

Bigfoot walking down the road out there in the Badlands on his way to your house in South Dakota."

I gave Chooch another look. He shivered because it was a look he had seen on his mother's face many times. It was a look that said, "You best watch yourself, young man."

Chooch knew when it was time to be quiet.

This was such a time.

"We're about a half hour from Indianapolis," said Uncle Jack. "That's where we'll be spending the night."

"Gather up your things and pick up any trash around you," Uncle Dynamite said, stretching his arms up and yawning loudly. "I want to get right into our room and get some shut-eye."

The Fix Is In

Dr. Almasty and His Henchmen

One week earlier, Dewdrop Inn, Asheville, North Carolina

"Hello... Hello! Can you hear me?"

Dr. Viktor Almasty pressed the phone to his ear with his left hand and pulled at the gray hairs of his beard with his right. The hotel room was hot, and the air was thick with humidity and the perfume the last occupant had worn.

"Who is this?" the voice on the other end of the line asked in a slow Southern drawl. "Is this one of those robocalls? I'm not interested."

"No, Seymour, it's not a robocall. It's me, Viktor." Dr. Almasty closed his eyes and rubbed the back of his neck.

"Viktor who?" Senator Seymour Payne asked, barely hiding his annoyance. He had stepped out of a committee hearing at the state capitol in Raleigh to take this call and now he regretted it. He should have just turned off his ringer in the first place.

"Viktor Almasty. Your former brother-in-law. I was married to your sister," Dr. Almasty sputtered with barely concealed rage. "You were a groomsman at my wedding, for Pete's sake!"

"Okay, Viktor, calm down," the senator said. "What do you need? I'm a very busy man, you know. I have a legislative committee to run. Important legislation to write. Very busy."

"Yes, I know how important you are, Seymour," Dr. Almasty said. "That's why I'm calling. What do you know about Judaculla Rock?"

"What? That boulder with the graffiti on it over near you?"

"They're petroglyphs," Dr. Almasty corrected him. "And it's a protected site. What would it take to get rid of those pesky state protections so some enterprising person could buy the site and develop the land around it?"

"That would require a change to state law—why? Who wants to build houses there?"

"Not houses—a mining operation. A big one," Dr. Almasty said. "There's a lot of gold in those hills, ready for the taking. I just need to get that land."

"Where would you get the money to buy the land and set up a gold-mining operation? That would cost millions—and the last I knew, you were teaching at a community college and living in an old shack in the woods."

"Never you worry, Seymour. I'm about to be very rich and I'm looking for a way to invest my millions and make them grow," Dr. Almasty said.

"In that case, a change in state law is very possible," Senator Payne said. Dr. Almasty could almost hear his ex-brother-in-law's pudgy hands rubbing together with greed. "As the chairman of the state historic preservation committee and the second (maybe third) most powerful man at the state capitol, I can make it happen with just a few words in the right ears. But it will cost you."

"How much?" Dr. Almasty asked, with a grimace. He could feel his stomach start to clench.

"I think a million would do it," Senator Payne said. "In advance."

Dr. Almasty sat in stunned silence, the kind of silence that makes politicians nervous.

"Hello? Viktor? You still there?"

"One million dollars. In advance," Dr. Almasty repeated. "Done."

"Pleasure doing business with you, brother," Senator Payne said. "Gotta run back into my committee hearing. Busy man, you know."

The senator hung up without saying goodbye.

Dr. Almasty looked across the hotel room at his reflection in the grimy mirror above the dresser. He could swear he had aged thirty years during that phone call.

He'd better find that Cherokee gold fast and lock Seymour into their deal.

Time to go back down to the Treasure Hunters Convention in the hotel ballroom and find some helpers. He couldn't do this alone.

The Journey Ends— for Now

Janees Hollow Horn

Back in the car, Tuesday

We left Indianapolis early the next day. Well, early for us. It was still morning anyway. Barely.

The miles rattled by in our old car. The trip seemed to take forever. I just wanted it to be over. We were going to run out of comic books soon and I couldn't stand the twangy noise coming from the front seat.

Uncle Jack and Uncle Dynamite were singing along with a guy who was in some jailhouse now, apparently for playing cards and shooting dice. I have no idea where playing games is illegal. A lot of these country songs seemed to have nonsense lyrics. Uncle Dynamite was wearing his black cowboy hat today, with his hair pulled back in a bushy gray ponytail. Because he was so tall, the top of the hat pushed against the roof of the car. He looked like one of those old statues from our history books, the ones that held up those Greek temples.

"What's so funny?" Chooch asked, looking up from his phone. I must have been smiling, thinking about statues of my uncles holding up a Greek building.

"Nothing," I said.

"I thought you were just amused by our uncles' singing," Chooch said.

I like my cousin, but he can be pretty thick sometimes.

"Singing?" I said. "I thought we had run over a cat or something. I was about to call 9-1-1 and report a hit-and-run."

Chooch reached over to the pile of comics scattered around me and grabbed a copy of *Lumberjanes*.

"You'll like that," I told him. "It's about a bunch of girls having adventures. And there are monsters!"

Yep, I really get my cousin, even if he sometimes doesn't seem to get me. But I knew I had him at monsters.

Uncle Dynamite had stopped singing. And I soon

saw why. He leaned back over the front seat and said, "Hey, Chooch, siqua hawiya aquaduli. Hand me some of that sausage."

Chooch reached into the back of the wagon and flipped the cooler open. He grabbed a bag of sausage slices and cheese chunks, shook off the water, and handed the bag to my uncle.

"Wado, Chooch!" Uncle Dynamite said, before he dug in.

"Want a soda while I'm in here?" Chooch asked me.

"Nah, then I'll just have to pee every five miles," I said, smiling.

He flipped back around and picked up his comic. "How much longer?" he asked my uncles. "My butt is getting sore from sitting in this car."

My uncles both laughed. Then Uncle Dynamite burped. Loudly. My uncles laughed again even harder.

"A few more miles," Uncle Jack said. "When Dynamite's burps get unbearable, we'll be just about there. Now, brother, hand me a hunk of that cheese," he said, looking hungrily at the snack bag in Uncle Dynamite's lap.

Chooch and I groaned and pulled our shirts up over our noses and mouths.

I had finished my last comic book somewhere in

Kentucky, so the last three or four hours had been spent watching videos on my phone and half listening to my uncles' stories. Chooch mostly kept to himself, occasionally shifting in his seat and telling me to get on my own side.

Just when I thought I couldn't spend one more minute in the car, we finally pulled into Western Carolina University. The college seemed to be built into the hills we had been driving through the past few hours. Woods surrounded the small campus. We could see mountains in every direction. I could almost imagine myself coming to college in a place like this. For some reason, this area just felt like home. I guess it was home for us at one time.

"We need to sign in at the Ramsey Regional Activity Center," Uncle Dynamite said, reading from a wrinkled piece of paper he pulled from his bag and shaking me out of my daydream.

"That's what I put in my GPS," Uncle Jack said. "It should take us right there."

He patted the dashboard and leaned down every now and then to try to read the names of the buildings we were passing.

The college campus was pretty empty. Only a few kids were walking around, along with small groups of elders.

"Where is everybody?" my cousin asked.

"It's summer, Chooch. School is out except for a few summer classes—and our symposium," Uncle Jack said.

Symposium. That's what the plant thing with all the boring talks was called—a symposium. Grandma said that word meant "Where's the coffee?" in Greek. I'm not sure if she was serious or not. I looked over at Chooch and he nodded. He must have read my mind.

We walked into the Ramsey Center, a big dark glass building shaped like the mountains around us.

It was cool in the building. Several people stood in line at the registration table. Others stood in groups, talking and laughing. There weren't any other kids.

I looked at Chooch and he shrugged.

Uncle Dynamite threw his arms wide and announced to no one in particular, "Your storytellers have arrived."

Uncle Jack chuckled. "Yeah, let the lies begin."

An elderly lady came rushing over. She was all smiles and dressed like she was going on a safari—khaki from head to toe and a million pockets. Her gray hair was cut short and pulled back with barrettes that had purple flowers on them.

"You must be our storytellers, the Bunches," she

said, shaking hands with Uncle Dynamite and Uncle Jack.

"Yep, two Bunches, a Tenkiller and a Hollow Horn," Uncle Jack said, sweeping his hand in an arc to pull Chooch and me into the conversation.

"I'm Dr. Millie Spooner, one of the organizers," the nice lady said. She looked more like a tall bird than a spoon. A tall bird going on a safari.

I made my hand into the shape of a bird and showed it to Chooch behind my back. He giggled and said, "Hesdi. Cut it out."

Hesdi was a word we both knew as the children of Cherokee mothers. That and etlawei, which meant "be quiet." And when Mom said that, you'd better be quiet and listen up.

"Is there someplace close by we can grab a bite to eat after we get registered?" Uncle Jack asked, rubbing his big belly.

"Oh, you're already registered," Dr. Spooner said, patting his arm and looking down at him. "You and your family are our honored guests. We'll be serving food in the dining hall after we get you settled in your rooms. You'll be staying in one of our residence halls, but let me assure you, the rooms are very comfortable."

She was right. The rooms were great, except

Chooch and I had to share one. I knew from sharing the hotel room with him and my uncles last night that Chooch snored—almost as loudly as Uncle Dynamite. I wouldn't be getting any sleep until we got back to Minneapolis, thanks to Cousin Thunder Boy.

"I get the top bunk," he said.

"Fine," I replied. "I prefer the lower bunk. Closer to the bathroom and the TV."

I threw my bag on the bed.

"Let's go eat, cuz," Chooch said. "We need to get to that cafeteria before Uncle Jack eats all the bacon cheeseburgers."

We ran out the door, down a winding path, and smacked into a group of men standing outside the cafeteria talking softly to one another. I plowed into the tallest man so hard he almost toppled over like a dead pine tree. A big man with a gray beard and tinted glasses put out his hands and stopped Chooch from knocking into him. He grabbed Chooch's arms and held him at a distance. I guess we must have startled them when we shot out of our room like two calves blasting down a rodeo chute.

"Hey, you kids watch where you're going!" the bearded man said in a gravelly voice. He was also dressed like he was going on a safari, but his safari shirt was stretched tighter over his middle than Dr.

Spooner's had been. And he didn't seem nearly as nice as the Bird Lady.

"Sorry," I said as we shook ourselves loose and ran past the men.

"Sheesh," Chooch said to me once we were out of earshot. "They think they own the place."

"Who thinks they own the place?" Uncle Dynamite asked loudly as he came around the corner with Uncle Jack. The men at the end of the hall looked our way. Uncle Dynamite waved to them. They just glared back.

"Friendly fellows," Uncle Dynamite said in a quieter voice. "I hope they're not in the front row for our storytelling tomorrow, Jack."

"Ain't that the truth? Well, I'm not gonna let the local welcoming committee spoil my appetite. Let's find that dining hall and get our feed bags on," Uncle Jack said. "Then, if there's time before it gets dark, I'd love to take a trip up to Judaculla Rock. Maybe get a glimpse of Bigfoot."

"Hawa!" Uncle Dynamite said before trotting down the hallway like a little kid. "Try to keep up!"

Uncle Jack put an arm over each of our shoulders and started slowly walking after his brother.

"No need to run—I'm hungry, kids, but I ain't that hungry," he said.

As if to contradict him, his stomach growled loudly.

"Ah, etlawei," he said, laughing.

THE ROCK

Chooch Tenkiller

You've never seen four people eat and drink so fast and so much. Cheeseburgers, fries, soda. Even my favorite, carrot cake, for dessert.

We ate so quickly I don't think any of us even stopped to take a breath. You'd think all the restaurants between Minneapolis and Cullowhee, North Carolina, were closed and we hadn't eaten in days.

But really, my uncles ate fast because they were anxious about getting up to Judaculla Rock before dark. And Janees and I, well, we were growing kids. We always ate that way.

We cleared our tables and looked around at the other people from the conference. They were spread out, sitting in small groups around the dining hall, talking quietly and eating slowly. Definitely a different sort of people.

"Race you to the car, Tsaquolade!" Uncle Dynamite said, using Uncle Jack's Indian name, which is pronounced jah-GWO-lah-day. It means "bluebird." And it's where his nickname, Jack, comes from.

Uncle Jack snorted in a most un-bluebird sort of way.

"Not likely, Harold. I've got the car keys and no one's going anywhere until I get there."

The fifteen-minute drive up the mountain might seem boring to some people. There were actually farms and cows on both sides of the road. But the mountains in the distance, all the rivers and streams, the deep forests...they were really kind of beautiful. We stopped at a pull-off to walk down to see the river. The brown water roared by, leaving white, foamy trails where the river creased the top of a rock or tumbled down a stone ledge. It was amazing to see: powerful, noisy—almost as if the river was alive, as my uncles always tell me it is.

"That's Caney Fork—it runs into the Tuckasegee River," Uncle Dynamite said. Uncle Jack tried to take a selfie with his phone. I tried not to laugh. His selfies always turned out funny—mostly blurry pictures of his thumb and half a face. He emailed them to everyone anyway.

We piled back in the car and continued our winding drive up the hill. Just when I thought the road would end and we would drive our beaten-up orange station wagon into the woods, Uncle Jack pulled to the side of the road. He leaned around the driver's seat and looked Janees and me in the eye.

"We're here. Now, remember. This place is sacred —it belongs to a spirit being. No horsing around, you two."

Janees and I looked at each other, then back at Uncle Jack. "Okay," I said. "We get it. Best behavior."

We got out of the car and stretched our legs. Uncle Dynamite opened the back hatch and pulled out a small leather pouch. It's where he kept his tobacco. He would be leaving some here for the spirit beings. It's an Indian thing. It's kind of like writing someone a thank-you note.

Across the road from the car I could see a fenced-in grassy area. Down the hill was a wooden walkway in the shape of a half circle with stone pillars and wooden rails. At the center of the half circle was a rock. Judaculla Rock was almost as big as our car. It looked like it was half sticking out of the ground, rounded and gray. The side facing the wooden walkway was flat and filled with carvings and deep indentations. It looked like someone had used it as a message board for thousands of years. Yup, must be the place.

My head started to tingle as I stood in the afternoon sun. I thought I heard voices floating on the breeze, but there were no other visitors as we walked down a long path to the walkway entrance. Must be the long ride catching up with me and the hot sun giving me the willies.

"Is this poison ivy?" Janees asked, pointing at a plant leaning out over the path as she leaned away from it with a funny expression on her face.

"No, that's wild grapes," Uncle Dynamite said. "That's an important plant. You can drink water from it if you ever get lost in the woods. And that one is pokeweed. The one with the orange flower over there is called jewelweed. All these plants are medicines for us, if you know how to use them."

"They can be poisonous if you don't," Uncle Jack warned.

Got it. We were surrounded by poisonous plants. Great. More important cultural education.

We kept walking down the path, stopping to read the big metal signs that told about the rock, the plants around the rock, and one about Judaculla himself. The signs were in English and in Cherokee. On one sign, there was a picture of a big man with long flowing hair carrying a deer over his shoulders.

"Holay—they made him look like Fabio, that Italian model guy with the long hair," said Uncle Jack, pointing at the picture. "You know, the one on the cover of all the romance novels. They must have thought Tsul'kalu was a white fellow for some reason."

Uncle Dynamite snickered. "You read romance novels, brother? I find out something new about you on every trip."

Uncle Jack turned red.

I had no idea who this Fabio guy was, but if he looked anything like this drawing, I felt sort of sorry for him.

We walked up to the middle of the walkway and got a closer look at the rock. There were markings and pictures all over the part facing us. It was like a huge blackboard with some sort of math equations or science formulas all over it. I don't know how anyone could tell what it said or what the pictures meant. I did see the seven-fingered handprint my uncle mentioned.

My head started to tingle again. I rubbed the back of my sweaty neck. Then I heard the voices again.

"Does anyone else hear that?" I asked.

"Hear what, neff?" Uncle Dynamite said.

"Those voices. It almost sounds like they're speaking Cherokee off in the distance. But I can't make out any of the words."

Both of my uncles stopped and listened to the breeze.

"I don't hear them," Uncle Jack said. "Dynamite, give him some of your tsolah. He should put some down if they're speaking to him."

Uncle Dynamite reached into his pants pocket and pulled out his small leather tobacco pouch. He put a pinch in my hand. "Go put it down by the rock," he said. "You should leave them something."

"Leave who something?" I asked him.

"The spirit beings. They're all around us here. We're in their home. We need to thank them for letting us be here and see this rock."

I knew my uncle was right. We are taught from a young age to respect the spirit world and to show our gratitude in the right way. That often means putting down some tobacco.

I put the tobacco on the edge of the walkway overlooking the rock and stepped back. In that moment, I felt a deep connection to my people and this place. Uncle Jack nodded.

"Can we go now?" Janees said. "I have to go to the

bathroom and I haven't seen any place with restrooms since we left the college."

"Yes, we've seen what we came to see today. We'll come back again before we head back to Minneapolis—and plan to spend some more time," Uncle Jack said. "We passed a gas station before we turned off the highway and came up the hill. We can stop there on the way back."

TREASURE HUNTERS JOIN FORCES

Dr. Almasty and His Henchmen

One week earlier, Dewdrop Inn,
Asheville, North Carolina

Dr. Almasty headed down to the ballroom on the main level. As he walked down the hallway toward the elevator, he wrinkled his nose at the wet, musty smell rising from the worn carpet. He could hear loud voices and discordant music coming from televisions and radios in the rooms he was walking past. The Dewdrop Inn was certainly not a Walt Disney World deluxe hotel. But it was cheap, which was the main draw for the Treasure Hunters Conference, he was sure.

As he walked into the ballroom, Dr. Almasty scanned the room for a seat away from the crowds. He

44

needed to do some people-watching with a purpose. He spied a cloth-covered bench against a back wall, next to a table with a large coffee pot and stacks of foam cups. He poured a cup of thick black coffee and sat down.

He almost gagged when he took his first sip of lukewarm, bitter coffee. It was as thick as molasses but not sweet in the slightest. It tasted a bit like liquid asphalt—or at least what he imagined liquid asphalt would taste like.

Dr. Almasty watched the conference attendees—amateur treasure hunters drawn to the area by stories of hidden caches of Cherokee gold. Almost all were men in their forties, fifties, or older. Most had unkempt hair, scruffy beards, or oddly shaped mustaches. They wore flannel shirts, or khaki outfits. Dr. Almasty himself favored khakis with lots of pockets. One could never have too many pockets.

The room was ringed with exhibit booths and display tables. The booths continued in two wide rows down the middle of the ballroom. Hawkers were showing off the latest metal detectors, sonar equipment, digital compasses, jackhammers, trowels, satellite radios, and any other tool or gadget the modern treasure hunter might need.

Dr. Almasty noticed a tall, thin man staring

intently at a table full of hand tools. He set down his coffee, heaved himself up and off the bench, and wandered over.

The tall, thin man, on closer inspection, had a nasty scar running down the side of his face. He was gently turning a long, menacing-looking knife over and over in his hands. He held the knife up to the light and looked down the length of its blade. Then he lowered the knife and hefted it in his palm, feeling its weight and testing its balance. He looked over at the booth attendant and said, "I'll take it."

"You have a good eye, my friend," the attendant said. "Why, this is our very finest Damascus steel—"

"Stow it," the thin man said. "I already bought the knife. Save the sales pitch for one of these other patsies."

The booth attendant reddened but didn't say another word. He slid the knife into its reddish-brown leather sheath and wrapped it in tissue paper before putting the bundle into a small white paper bag with rope handles.

"That'll be $350," he said, without looking the thin man in the eyes.

"I'll give you a hundred and you'll still make a handsome profit, you pirate," the thin man said, slapping down a $100 bill.

The booth attendant didn't argue. He just put the bill in his cash box and mumbled, "Have a good day."

As the thin man turned around, Dr. Almasty reached up and put a hand on his shoulder.

"You and I need to talk," Dr. Almasty said. "I think you're just the sort of fellow I'm looking for. My name is Dr. Viktor Almasty, but you can call me Dr. Almasty."

"What sort of fellow are you looking for, Viktor?"

Dr. Almasty cringed. "It's Dr. Almasty. I'm looking for some partners. I know how to find a cache of Cherokee gold and I need a couple of able-bodied partners to get it. We'll split the find evenly and all be rich. Interested?"

The tall man looked down at the bearded man, trying to figure out if he really had a lead on the gold or if he was just another one of these cranks. "My name is Nuppence. I've been looking for the gold since I got out—er, for a few years now. My, um, roommate at the last place I stayed kept talking about this Cherokee gold. Figured it was somewhere up near the Tennessee-North Carolina line. But I haven't had much luck on my own. Let's talk."

The two men wandered out of the ballroom and took facing seats in a small alcove nearby. They kept their voices low, but shared just enough of what they knew to keep the other interested. They talked for almost an hour, until their conversation was interrupted by a loud disturbance back by the doors to the ballroom.

A pair of beefy security guards in dark blue coats and gray slacks were trying to subdue a short, stout man with bushy eyebrows. The short man, who had a long leather tube strapped to his back, writhed and yelled, "You have to let me in! I'm a presenter. I'm an expert at finding hidden treasure. I know where the Cherokee gold is! I have maps!"

Both guards kept shouting, "No admission without a badge."

The three men squirmed and wrestled, but the stout man, who was wearing a loud purple Hawaiian shirt and dingy white painter's pants, would not be contained.

The stout man broke free from the security guards, who fell to the floor in a tangle. He dashed down the hallway toward Nuppence and Dr. Almasty.

As he passed the seated men, the stout man gave them a smile and a wink. "Gentlemen," he said, tipping his nonexistent hat to them as he ran toward the escalator like a purple lightning bolt.

Nuppence looked at Dr. Almasty, who said, "Are you thinking what I'm thinking?" Nuppence nodded and the two men were off, chasing the stout man down the escalator and out the front door.

"Wait—you there in the purple shirt—wait!" Dr. Almasty shouted after the short man.

When they rounded the side of the building and ran into the parking lot, the short man slowed at last. He came to a stop and turned to face the two pursuers. He put his hands on his knees and panted and huffed, trying to catch his breath.

"What do you two mugs want?" he asked between gulps of air. "If you're here to rob me, I should warn you that I know karate."

"We just wanna talk," Nuppence said.

"We're looking for a partner in our gold-hunting venture," Dr. Almasty said. "And it sounds like you might be a prime candidate, if what you said back there about being an expert in the Cherokee treasure was true."

"Oh, it's true all right," said the stout man, finally catching his breath and pointing with a pudgy thumb to the tube over his shoulder. "And I have the maps to prove it. I'm selling them for one hundred bucks each. But today only, they're five for $600."

He held out a pudgy hand and said, "Name's Dottle. And you just found yourselves a partner. Now let's get out of here!"

8

THE LITTLE PERSON

Chooch Tenkiller

In the forest near Cullowhee,
North Carolina,
Wednesday, late morning

The next morning, everyone at the conference went on field trips around the college, just like they were back in middle school. Only these field trips were actually hikes in the fields nearby. And the woods. Some people even just walked around the campus. All the field trips were just to look at plants.

I'm not kidding. I love nature and the beauty of the outdoors; I just can't take people talking about it all the time. Sometimes you just have to be in nature. Appreciate it. Admire it. Quietly.

But today, the whole day was to be one long, sweaty plant hunt leading up to the big event after dinner:

Cherokee stories around the bonfire with Jack and Dynamite Bunch.

My uncles decided to join everyone else and look at plants. They dragged Janees and me along with them and about a dozen other elderly people to look at medicine plants in a nearby forest.

"These are our medicine plants, you two," Uncle Jack said. "Pay attention. You might learn something that will save your life one day."

That was doubtful. But at least we would be outside and not cooped up in that car or stuck in our room back at the college.

We walked along the forest path, listening to the old people talk about the plants we were passing and stepping on.

"Pssst, Chooch. Pssst," Janees said quietly.

"What? Can't you tell I'm really interested in this plant talk?" I rolled my eyes.

"Wanna do something fun?" she asked. "Let's explore a little. I think I hear a stream or a waterfall or something."

I started backing away from the group. None of the elders noticed us. They were all busy studying a bush of some kind. Janees turned and dashed into the trees along the path.

"C'mon," she said. "Let's see if we can find that waterfall. Maybe we can go swimming."

I wasn't sure that was a good idea—I mean, neither of us had a bathing suit on—but it was nice to be away from the science class.

We walked toward the sound of the water for quite a while, but we still couldn't see any river or falls.

"We shouldn't go too far, Janees," I said. "We don't want to get lost."

"Don't be a baby," she said. "We'll go back in a few minutes. Our uncles won't even know we're gone."

We came to a clearing with a few downed trees. I jumped up and sat on a big log that was held above the ground by two other trees. I wiped a hand across my sweaty forehead and rubbed my knees.

Janees sat at the other end of the log, about ten feet away.

"We used to live here," she said. "Cherokee people, I mean."

"Cherokee people still live here in North Carolina. I went to their reservation on a trip with Grandma and Mom a couple of years ago," I said. "You know we still have relatives here, right? They live in this place called Snowbird."

"Sounds cold," Janees said, as she wiped sweat off the back of her neck. "I could use a little cold right about now. Ready to go find that waterfall?"

But I didn't answer. I was too busy staring at the little man walking across the clearing toward us. He raised a hand to me, before hopping up on the log between Janees and me.

When I say he was little, I mean like a little kid. He wore a long-sleeved white shirt with an orange belt around his waist. He had on black pants, a blue turban, and—were those moccasins?

"We probably have time to swim before we head back," Janees said. "Chooch! Are you listening to me? You're always off in your own little world."

"Don't you see him, Janees?" I said, gesturing to the man sitting on the log between us.

"See who, you goof? Stop messing around and let's go find that waterfall before our uncles come find us and drag us back to Boredom City," Janees said.

The little man just shook his head.

"She can't see me, you know," he said quickly, putting a hand on my arm. "I'm here to talk to you. That's why you can see me. We don't have much time. So pay attention, atsutsa."

He called me atsutsa, which is the word for "young man" in the Cherokee language. It's pronounced ah-JOO-ja. It's where my nickname, Chooch, comes from.

But I'm getting off topic here. I mean, I was sitting next to a little man that only I could see! Either I was losing my mind or the summer heat was getting to me. Or there was one more possibility—all those stories about the Little People my uncles told were true and I was actually sitting next to one.

Couldn't be. Could it?

"I see you've figured it out, atsutsa," the Little Person said. "I'm exactly what you think I am."

I shook my head, trying to clear my mind and make this vision go away.

"Don't shake your head at me, Chooch Tenkiller," Janees said, hopping down from the log. "If you just want to sit here like a literal bump on a log, you go ahead. But I'm going to find that waterfall and go swimming."

She stomped off.

"Hawa, atsutsa, we don't have much time. We need your help," said the Little Person as he leaned toward me. "And this could get dangerous."

A shiver ran up my spine, even though it was hot and muggy in the clearing.

"How can I help you? I'm just a kid," I said. "And I'm not even from around here."

The Little Person looked me right in the eye. He smiled for the first time.

"You're not just a kid—you're THE kid. We have stories about you."

That was funny. We had stories about the Little People and they had stories about us.

Not us. *Me.* What the heck?

The Little Person reached into the beaded leather-and-cloth bag he carried across his right shoulder. He pulled out a leather-wrapped bundle. He carefully unfolded the leather to reveal the biggest jewel I had ever seen. It was like a clear diamond, but there was a red vein running through it. It threw off its own light, a light so bright I had to shade my eyes.

"Don't look directly at the crystal," the Little Person said. "It's called Ulvsati, the great transparent stone from Uktena, the great snake monster."

My head started to spin. I wasn't sure if it was the light from the stone, the heat, or this crazy story from a Little Person right out of one of my uncles' tales. I had to grab the log with both hands to keep from falling over. I squeezed the warm, rough bark.

"You need to take this crystal to Tsul'kalu's rock. We

saw you there with your family yesterday. When you get to the rock, unwrap Ulvsati, but don't let anyone see it, whatever you do. When you touch the crystal, you will see everything around you more clearly. Then you'll know what you're supposed to do."

I shook my head no.

"You'll have to tell me more than that. I'm just a kid. I can't go running around North Carolina looking at rocks and hiding magic crystals," I said. "You've obviously got the wrong kid. I'm no one special—just a boy from Minneapolis on a long road trip with his family."

Did he really think I could just drive myself to Judaculla Rock while Janees and my uncles sat around the residence hall playing Cribbage? I didn't even have my license yet. I couldn't even start driver's ed until the end of next school year.

I mean, come on.

The Little Person held out the bundle. He looked at me without moving or speaking.

Without thinking, I took the bundle from him. And that was it. He was gone. I don't mean he turned, waved, and walked away. He was just gone and I was holding a leather bundle with a big rock in it.

So I did what any kid would do: I stuck it in my

backpack with all my other stuff. I hopped down from the log just in time to meet Janees coming up the path.

She did not look cool and refreshed. She looked kind of mad.

"There's no stupid waterfall anywhere around here," she said. "I can't even hear it anymore, can you?"

No, I couldn't. But what I could hear was Uncle Jack's booming voice. And he didn't sound happy, either.

"Chooch! Janees! Where the heck are you two? Dehena! Come here!"

"Stay with us, you two," Uncle Dynamite said as he and Uncle Jack walked into the clearing and saw us. "Jack and I want to get back to the college so we can make one more run up to the rock before we have to tell stories around the bonfire tonight. Let's go back and rejoin the group."

My backpack suddenly felt heavy.

And I could swear it was humming.

TREASURE HUNTERS PLAN

Dr. Almasty and His Henchmen

In a cabin in the
Balsam Mountains,
Wednesday, early afternoon

"Almasty, how do you know the gold is hidden in these hills?" the tall, thin man with a scar down the left side of his face asked in an accent that was definitely not Southern.

"That's Dr. Almasty, Nuppence. Doctor. How many times do I have to tell you?" the bearded man said sharply. He let out a deep breath, leaned back in his chair, and put his hands behind his head. His weight caused the chair to groan in pain. He shuffled his body around in the seat to keep from tipping over, then shot the other men a look that warned them not to say anything about his weight. "Like I told you at the Treasure Hunters Conference, I know the gold is here, Nuppence, because I grew up here. I heard all the stories about the Cherokee and their gold when I was a boy. Those greedy Indians kept it all for themselves and hid it from us. I'm here to take what's rightfully mine."

"Theirs, you mean," said the short, stout man with thick eyebrows and a crooked smile. "It's theirs, but it's going to be ours."

"Shut up, Dottle. No one asked you," Dr. Almasty snapped.

The short man shrugged. He took a sip from his coffee and looked down at the pile of paper in front of him.

"Why did you even come along on this treasure hunt if you didn't think there was a treasure here for the taking, Dottle?" Dr. Almasty asked. "Or you, Nuppence. Why are you here if you're doubting the existence of the gold? When we met at that treasure hunters gathering at that crummy hotel in Asheville, you both signed up for the job."

Nuppence and Dottle looked at each other, then back to Dr. Almasty.

"You know we aren't the only ones looking for it," Dr. Almasty continued. "People have been crawling over these hills with shovels and pickaxes since we drove those Cherokee savages to Oklahoma nearly two hundred years ago. If you don't believe the gold is hidden here, then go find another group of treasure hunters and look somewhere else."

"We believe you," Dottle said. "Take it easy."

"Yeah, we just have questions and want to make sure we're treated as equals," Nuppence said. "You owe us that. You said you wanted partners, not employees."

The three men settled into an awkward silence.

They sat around a rough wooden table in a small, dark room in Dr. Almasty's cabin. Nuppence was using a whetstone to hone the mean-looking knife he had bought at the conference. The dirty wooden walls of the cabin were unbroken on three sides. On the fourth was the door and a small window with cracked, yellowed glass. The window was so dirty that no one could see in or out. A wood stove in the corner had a fire smoldering in it, even though it was summer.

On the table in front of the men were a pile of yellowed maps, rulers, and a stubby pencil. A small spiral-bound notebook lay open on top of the maps. Scrawled on its pages were notes, pictures, rough maps, and a sketch of the markings from Judaculla Rock. A few of the pages were crossed out with big red Xs. Others had been scribbled out in pencil.

"Well, Dottle, this is when your expertise is really needed," Dr. Almasty said. "You're the map expert.

Where should we be looking?"

Dottle looked down at the maps on the table, then back up at Dr. Almasty. Nuppence paused his knife sharpening and cleared his throat in a grunt that sounded more like a threat.

"Well, you guys, uhm, you know how it is," Dottle started. "When I said I was an expert back at the conference, that was really just part of my sales pitch. I mean, I really want to find the gold—who wouldn't? But I was at the conference to sell maps, not to read them."

The other two men glared at Dottle and shook their heads. Nuppence held up his knife, which gleamed menacingly in the light, but Dr. Almasty stopped him.

"Just as I suspected all along, Dottle," Dr. Almasty said, eerily calm. "You're nothing but a two-bit con man. Since you can't actually read a treasure map, we'll just have to find another way to make you useful. You can cook for us. Drive the truck. Haul boxes up and down stairs. In other words, you're not brains—you're strictly…my flunky!"

Dottle turned red and looked down at the table.

Almasty—Dr. Almasty, rather—leaned forward and picked up the pencil and notebook. He flipped the page and touched the tip of the pencil lead to his tongue.

He began to write.

"We're going to need some things," he said, looking up at Nuppence and Dottle.

"What things?" Nuppence asked.

"Supplies and such. I have a feeling we're close—even without Dottle's blasted map. I can feel it in my bones. I've been looking for so long, we're bound to find the gold soon. We'll need shovels, a dolly, a couple of lengths of rope, duffel bags."

Dr. Almasty ticked the items off his list.

"How are we paying for all these supplies?" Nuppence asked. "We're broke. What are we gonna do? Rob a bank?"

"You let me worry about that," Dr. Almasty said. "That's my job. Like I said, I'm the brains of this operation. You're the brawn and Dottle is the...the... well, I'll figure out some menial tasks for him. So be quiet and go lift something heavy, or whatever it is you do."

Nuppence just stared at Dr. Almasty.

"How do you know we're close?" Dottle asked. He was at least a full step behind the others in the conversation.

Nuppence and Dr. Almasty turned and looked at him.

"Shut up, Dottle," they said in unison.

Dr. Almasty flipped back to an earlier page and studied the sketch of Judaculla Rock. He reached into his coat pocket and pulled out an old, dented magnifying glass. He moved it over the sketch, peering at each of the markings.

"The secret is here somewhere," he said to no one in particular. "I know this blasted rock is a map to that Cherokee gold. That's what the stories say. The answer is right in front of our eyes. What is it? Tell me your secret, you confounded rock."

Dottle looked at Dr. Almasty curiously.

"Why are you talking to the rock? It can't hear you. I mean, it's just a picture of the rock. Isn't it?"

"Shut up, Dottle," the other two men said again in unison.

"You know, I am getting tired of you guys ganging up on me," Dottle said. "One day I might just…might just…might…punch you in the nose."

Nuppence scoffed. Dr. Almasty ignored Dottle's threat, rolled up the maps, and carried them over to a black leather tube standing in the corner of the cabin. He walked back to the table, straightened the books, and stuck the pencil into the spiral rings of the notebook. Then he tucked the notebook into his jacket pocket, along with the magnifying glass, and cleared his throat.

Dottle and Nuppence stood up. Dottle carried the coffee mugs over to the sink, then scurried back to the table. He stood next to Nuppence, awaiting orders. Dr. Almasty still stood at the table. Gripping the edge, he stared into the distance, as if seeing something the others couldn't.

"We need to go back to the rock," he said. "I need to see it. I need to study it in person. I need to listen to it—make it tell me its secrets."

Nuppence and Dottle looked at each other behind Dr. Almasty's back. Dottle raised an eyebrow. Nuppence rolled his eyes. That made Dottle snort.

"What are you laughing at, dummy?" Dr. Almasty turned and glared at Dottle.

"Nothing." The short man stared down at his dirty boots.

"I thought so," Dr. Almasty said. "So shut your trap and go get the truck started. I want to get up to the rock before dark."

Dottle looked at Nuppence. Nuppence gave him a slight nod and Dottle turned to walk out the front door.

"I'm not sure how much longer I'm going to stick

this out without a payday," Nuppence said.

"We're almost there, boyo. Don't quit on me now," Dr. Almasty replied. "When we find that hidden gold, every day will be a payday for us. I'm going to use the money to buy that blasted Judaculla Rock and all the land around it and dig the world's largest gold mine. It will be beautiful: pits and tunnels in every direction, as far as the eye can see. Beautiful."

Nuppence squinted at Dr. Almasty.

"And how do you think you're going to do that? The rock is a national park or a historic site or whatever," he sneered. "They're not going to let you just buy it and start digging mine shafts."

Dr. Almasty chuckled slyly.

"I have a way, don't you worry," he said, patting Nuppence on the shoulder just a little too hard. "My brother-in-law is a bigwig in the state legislature. He said he can remove any protections Judaculla Rock has at any time. For a price."

The Rock Speaks

Chooch Tenkiller

Our car bounced its way up the road. My uncles were quiet, watching the scenery pass by. Janees let her eyes close and leaned her head back against the seat. Our supper of catfish, greens, and hush puppies was making me a little sleepy, too.

But I couldn't relax for long.

Hmmmmmmmmmm.

I could swear my backpack was still vibrating, like my phone when it's set to silent mode.

Hmmmmmmmmmm.

All I could think about was the shiny crystal wrapped in its leather hide. How was I ever going to pull it out of my bag and hold it up to Judaculla Rock without anyone noticing? I mean, I had a hard enough time just sitting on the couch at home minding my own business, without Mom noticing and telling me to go mow the lawn or pick up my room.

Stealthy and sneaky I'm not. I'm just a regular kid.

A regular kid who sees Little People.

"Just about to the turnoff up the hill. Last chance to use an indoor bathroom," Uncle Jack said. "Anyone gotta pee? We're not coming back down the mountain for a while."

Janees opened her eyes and shook her head no.

"Nah, I'm good," I said.

Hmmmmmmmmm.

Did no one else hear that? Apparently not.

We parked in the same spot along the road as last time. Ours was the only car around. I didn't see any people. Guess we would have the rock to ourselves. At least for now.

We all hopped out of the car. We walked down the path toward the raised walkway around the boulder. This time we didn't have to stop to read every sign. At least that was something to be thankful for.

Hmmmmmmmmmm.

Yes, crystal, I remember you're in there.

When we got to the middle of the walkway, my uncles put down tobacco for the rock. They bowed their heads and each spoke softly in the Cherokee language. Janees and I stood back and stayed quiet. I didn't know what they were saying exactly, but Janees and I knew enough to show them respect.

Uncle Dynamite had an old camera with a long lens hanging on a leather strap around his neck. He took off the lens cap, fiddled with the lens, and snapped a series of pictures of the rock. Uncle Jack pulled out a long spiral notebook, unhooked a ballpoint pen from its spirals, and began to jot down his observations.

"What do you think, brother?" Uncle Jack said. "Does this hunk of soapstone tell us how to find Bigfoot at last?"

Uncle Dynamite ran his hand over his chin absentmindedly. He would have stroked his whiskers if he had any. But none of the Bunch or Tenkiller men had much (or any) facial hair. My dad got me an electric razor for my thirteenth birthday last year, but I don't think I'll ever need to take it out of its box.

"Tlayaquanta... I don't know," Uncle Dynamite finally answered. "I just don't know. I can't make anything out from any of these carvings. Just looks like a lot of random lines and stick figures to me."

"Do you see anything, Chooch? Janees?" Uncle Jack asked, waving the two of us over to the railing. "You young people have better eyes than us old guys. Purer spirits, too. Means you can see things our eyes are too clouded to see or our minds are too closed to believe."

"That's why children can sometimes see the Little People, but adults usually can't," Uncle Dynamite added.

My heart jumped and I almost blurted out my story.

Almost.

Instead, I just nodded and rubbed a hand over my nonexistent chin whiskers.

"Well, you both have been pretty well-behaved and respectful while your uncle and I looked at our rock and paid our respects to the spirit beings, so we have a surprise," Uncle Jack said. "We asked the nice lady at the dining hall to pack us a special treat to enjoy while we're up here on the mountain. I haven't opened the box yet, but I think I got a whiff of fresh-baked pie when I stuck it in the back."

Janees clapped her hands. My stomach growled in reply.

Uncle Jack walked back to the car and grabbed the pie box, a pile of paper plates, a box of plastic forks, and a kitchen knife he must have had tucked away somewhere.

While Uncle Jack was taking his pie hike, Uncle Dynamite opened his pack and pulled out a colorful wool blanket. We walked down a path away from the rock in hopes of finding some shade. When we found a suitable spot, Uncle Dynamite spread out his blanket and said, "Y'all have a seat." Janees and I plopped down and waited for our pie.

The pie was worth the wait. It was double-crusted and filled with fat, dark berries.

"Alisdayvdi," Uncle Jack said. "Time to eat."

We tucked into the pie and actually ate the whole thing, just the four of us. I was pretty proud of our effort when we were done.

Uncle Jack and Uncle Dynamite lay back on the blanket, each putting his hands behind his head. They looked up as white, puffy clouds drifted lazily across the sky.

"You know, pie like that makes a fellow a little nappy," Uncle Dynamite said. "Hawaga? Isn't that right, Jack?"

"Hawa! Feeling a bit warm and nappy myself."

Both of my uncles closed their eyes. They started to breathe deeply, almost snoring when they exhaled.

"Wanna go look at the rock some more?" I asked Janees.

"Nah, I think I'm going to walk off some of that pie and see what's a little farther down this path. I think I hear some water again. Maybe this time I'll actually find it."

"All right. But don't go too far," I said as I grabbed my backpack and walked toward the walkway and Judaculla Rock.

I looked all around. No one was coming.

I set down my backpack and stared at the big gray rock.

"Stop your humming," I said to the backpack. "I'm here. I'm doing what the Little Person said. So just etlawei!"

Sheesh. I was starting to sound like my grandma.

I nudged the backpack with my sneaker. The top flopped open and the leather bundle rolled out.

I picked it up, unwrapped the leather, and grabbed the crystal inside.

Wham!

My whole world changed in an instant. Light flashed and colored the whole world a greenish blue.

I don't even remember dropping the hide onto my backpack.

As my vision cleared, I saw Little People all around me. They were sitting on tree branches, standing along the walkway, walking up the road. The air was electric—it made the hairs on my neck stand up and I could see small blue sparks where my fingers gripped the crystal.

Then I saw him.

Who, you ask?

Him. Bigfoot. Tsul'kalu. Whatever you want to call him.

I mean, you couldn't miss him. He must be ten feet tall and covered in hair. It was like *poof!* and he was standing six feet away from me at the railing. He raised his massive hand with seven fingers and nodded to me.

"Osiyo, atsutsa," he said in a voice that sounded like thunder rolling through the valley around us. "Hello, son. Tsul'kalu daquadoa. They call me Tsul'kalu."

I just stood there with my mouth hanging open. My heart was hammering in my chest. My ears buzzed. I felt like I might pass out. The only sound I could make was a low wheeze as I slowly backed up a few steps.

"Look at my rock," he said, waving his hand toward the boulder. "What do you see?"

When I looked at the rock, I almost fainted. What had been flat carvings on a gray stone were now a three-dimensional scene with people, animals, and other creatures. And not only that—they were moving! It was like the markings were actually alive.

"Whoa!" I said. "Next thing you know they'll be talking to me."

Tsul'kalu smiled. "So you've seen this before?"

"What?"

But he didn't have a chance to answer.

"Siyo, boy." One of the markings, shaped sort of like a jellyfish, was talking to me. I could hear singing—a stomp dance song. I felt faint again.

"I know this is a lot to take in, son."

My knees started to feel wobbly and my whole head grew hot.

"I need you to listen to my rock," Tsul'kalu said. "There are people—bad people—who think that it is some sort of treasure map. It is and it isn't. We put it here as a message. It's a message about something we consider quite valuable, but it's not the sort of treasure the bad men seek."

"What message?"

"Watch. Just watch."

I did.

I Spy with My Little Eye

Dr. Almasty and His Henchmen

Near Judaculla Rock, Wednesday,
late afternoon

"What's that kid doing?" Dr. Almasty held the binoculars to his eyes and gazed across the pasture at the walkway around the rock. A tall American Indian boy with a braided ponytail was holding some sort of glowing rock and talking to himself. What was this? Some sort of Indian ceremony?

"Are we going up to the rock or not?" Dottle asked. He and Nuppence leaned against the truck, which they had pulled into the shaded turnoff.

"Shut up, you fool," Dr. Almasty said. "Let me think."

"I told you to stop talking to me like that unless you want a black eye—or worse," Dottle said huffily.

Dr. Almasty waved a hand impatiently at the short man and turned his attention back to the scene at the rock.

Was the kid reading the rock out loud? Could it be? Was he some sort of mystical Indian shaman or something? He was just a kid.

"We're going to wait right here. Then we're going to follow that kid when he heads down the mountain. I'm going to find out what he knows and see if he can read that rock," Dr. Almasty said. "Boys, we might have finally gotten our break."

"And when you're done with him, he's mine," Nuppence said, patting the hunting knife he carried on his hip. "It's been a long time since I heard a kid scream."

Dottle didn't say anything, but his shudder said everything.

Uktena and His Crystal

Chooch Tenkiller

We were strangely quiet in the back seat on the way back to campus. Janees was sleeping, head lolled back, mouth wide open. I was sitting up in my seat, staring straight ahead, but not really looking at anything. I was trying to keep my face expressionless, and not look freaked out, but if someone looked closely, they could probably have seen the beads of sweat on my forehead.

After the late-afternoon pie feast, no one was particularly hungry, except for Uncle Jack, who said he could "eat a little something."

We ate a quick meal in the dining hall—slices of pizza for Uncle Dynamite, me, and Janees, and a fried chicken sandwich, fries, and a milkshake for Uncle Jack.

"Well, almost time to go out to the bonfire and tell stories," Uncle Dynamite said. "Know which ones you're telling tonight, Jack?"

"I'll probably tell a few rabbit trickster stories. You?"

"I'm going to tell an Uktena story, since we're near where it happened," Uncle Dynamite said. "Maybe tell how the hunter got Ulvsati and how he cares for it."

At that last bit, I snapped to attention. "How the hunter got what?"

"Ulvsati—the great crystal. That word means 'transparent,' but Uktena's crystal has a vein of blood running through it. The old people who've seen it say it gives off a bright light when it's held."

I shuddered and tried to swallow, but my throat was dry. I couldn't find the strength to ask any more questions, though I felt like I should have a million of them.

"Well, let's get going then," Uncle Jack said. "These lies aren't going to tell themselves."

The bonfire was burning brightly behind the dining hall. Someone had set up a coffee cart with an assortment of cookies. Uncle Jack walked over and grabbed a cup and a handful of cookies. Uncle Dynamite strode over to the fire and turned to face the gathered plant specialists.

"Siyo, nigadv. Dynamite Bunch daquadoa," he started. "Hi, everyone, my name is Dynamite Bunch. My brother, Jack, and I are here to tell you a little more about this place, the original homelands of our Cherokee people."

The audience clapped. Janees and I settled in on a log bench at the back of the crowd. I hadn't heard the story my uncle planned to tell tonight. But I was hoping to find out more soon about the crystal that hummed and glowed in the backpack back in my room.

"This is a story the old men told me when I was a boy," Uncle Dynamite started.

"We aren't sure when this story happened, but we know that it happened just about thirty miles up the river from where you're now sitting. After you hear it, you'll certainly be more careful when you're walking through the woods or swimming in the river.

"Uktena was a large snake, as big around as the biggest tree in the forest. It had horns on its head and a pair of wings. Spots ran from its head down its side. But its most distinguishing feature was a large diamond-like stone in the middle of its forehead.

"The old people say that to look directly at that stone could kill a hunter. Even to gaze upon Uktena while it slept could kill a hunter's entire family.

"Uktena hid along forest paths and lurked in the shallows of the streams and rivers near here, ambushing and eating anyone who stumbled upon it.

"One day, the people sent a conjurer they had captured in a battle to kill Uktena. In return for his life, this conjurer, who was called Groundhog's Mother, said he would rid the Cherokee of this great threat and bring home Uktena's crystal, called Ulvsati.

"So Groundhog's Mother made a perilous journey through the forests all around the Cherokee country, looking for Uktena. He encountered giant beasts of all sorts—green snakes, frogs, even fish—but none of these posed a threat to the Cherokee. Finally, he came upon Uktena sleeping on top of a mountain.

"Groundhog's Mother ran to the bottom of the mountain and built a large circle of fire. Then he notched an arrow and took aim at Uktena's heart, which was beneath the seventh spot from the snake's giant head. When the arrow struck it, the snake reared up and rushed down the mountain toward the conjurer.

"But the arrow had found its mark and Uktena died before it reached Groundhog's Mother, who had leapt across the fire and stood at a safe distance. The great snake writhed and spat poison all around as it died, but most of the poison was consumed by the ring of fire. Only one drop of poison struck Groundhog's Mother, on his forehead, but he did not feel it. But where the poison struck him, a small snake grew. Other people could see this snake, but Groundhog's Mother could not.

"Groundhog's Mother called all the birds of the forest to Uktena's carcass. He told them to eat their fill. When he returned seven days later, all of the snake was gone, even its bones.

"Then he saw something glowing like fire in the low branches of a tree. It was the great snake's crystal, Ulvsati. Groundhog's Mother wrapped the crystal in a deer hide and carried it back to the Cherokee people.

"The crystal gave Groundhog's Mother even greater magical power. He hid the crystal in a large pot and stashed it in a secret cave, where he had to return every seven days to feed it the blood from an animal. The crystal is still cared for by our relatives just west of here to this day. It still has tremendous power for our people. And that's the story of Uktena and its crystal. Wado."

The audience applauded.

I rubbed my forehead with my hands. What had I gotten myself into?

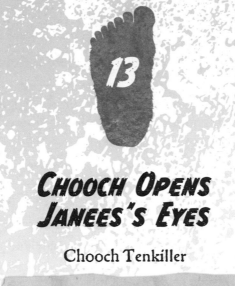

CHOOCH OPENS JANEES'S EYES

Chooch Tenkiller

I don't know how I slept last night. All I could think about was Uncle Dynamite's story and what Tsul'kalu's crystal had shown me. But I did sleep. A little. Now Janees and I are sitting in the back of a conference hall listening to my uncles tell more stories. I took a sip of my coffee. Ewww. I still couldn't get used to the taste of this stuff. I don't know how my uncles can drink so much of it—and seem to enjoy it.

"What are you doing, Chooch?" Janees scrunched up her nose and squinted at me.

"What do you mean, what am I doing? Sitting here, same as you."

"You don't drink coffee," she said.

"Yes, I do. Look at me drinking it," I boasted as I slurped a big gulp of black coffee. I almost gagged, of course.

Janees laughed.

"…Tsul'kalu, some people say, is as big as an oak tree." Uncle Jack was in the middle of a story. "Others say he is just a large man with long hair and a beard. None of us knows for sure. We just know that he is a giant."

Uncle Dynamite, who stood behind Uncle Jack in his cowboy hat and orange Pendleton jacket, nodded his head. "Hawa," he said.

"This giant roams these very hills, watching over this campus and this town," Uncle Jack continued. "Tsul'kalu has left his marks on a rock above this town, and in streambeds for miles around. Yet no one has seen him…"

I looked at Janees. I had to tell someone. I had to.

"Well, that part isn't true," I said.

"What?" Janees asked.

"Shhh!" whispered a lady at the next table, leaning

over and giving us a look.

I looked at Janees and rolled my eyes.

"Let's go outside for a while. Maybe we can find some food or something," I said.

Janees and I made our way out of the conference center and into the warm sunshine. We walked along the sidewalk, occasionally sniffing the air for doughnuts or biscuits.

"What were you talking about in there?" Janees said.

"I said it wasn't true that no one had seen Tsul'kalu."

"What are you talking about? The old days? Uncle Jack meant no one had seen him in modern times," Janees said.

"I saw him. Yesterday. At Judaculla Rock."

"Yeah, right," Janees said. "You're such a fibber. You're as bad as our uncles."

"I'm serious, cuz," I said, stopping in the middle of the sidewalk and looking into her eyes. "He spoke to me. Gave me a message. Well, the rock did. An important message. End of the world stuff. A scary message. But what am I supposed to do about it? I'm just a kid."

"You're not making any sense. Did you fall and hit your head or something?" Janees asked. "My dad's brother, Uncle Ty, talks like this when his blood sugar gets too low."

"I'm serious, cuz," I repeated. "And I can prove it."

I reached into my backpack and pulled out the leather bundle. I unfolded it and touched the crystal. It lit up and sparks danced around my fingers. My head grew light and then I saw them: Little People were all around us. I quickly wrapped the crystal back up and put it away.

"What do you have there?" Janees asked. "Some kind of lantern or something?"

"We'd better sit down over here," I said, gesturing to a table and chairs outside a closed coffee shop.

We sat and I told Janees the whole story, starting with my meeting the Little Person on the plant field trip, the crystal, and my visit to the rock last evening. When I was through, Janees just stared at me, shaking her head from side to side.

"I don't believe you," she said. "You're just making up stories to see if I'm dumb enough to believe them."

I shook my head no.

"I wouldn't do that, Janees. I just needed someone I could talk to about all this. Someone I trust."

She still stared at me, shaking her head.

"Nice try, Chooch, but I'm not falling for this stuff."

So I had no choice. I had to do it.

I took the bundle from my backpack and slowly unwrapped the crystal. I held it out to Janees.

"Don't believe me? Just ask them—they'll tell you."

"Who'll tell me?" she asked as she took the crystal from me.

Blue sparks leapt from her fingers. She stopped shaking her head and stiffened.

"Oh. My. Stars! Where did all these Little People come from?"

They're After Me!

Chooch Tenkiller

Janees handed me the crystal.

"What is going on here?"

I put the crystal back in its bundle and stowed it in my bag.

"I told you. The Little Person gave me this crystal and told me to take it to Judaculla Rock. Yesterday, when we went up there to have our pie or whatever, I touched the crystal while I was looking at the rock, and Tsul'kalu was there.

Janees started shaking her head again.

"You can't tell anybody. Not even Uncle Jack or Uncle Dynamite. Nobody," I said. "I wasn't even supposed to tell you. But I had to tell someone. Just so I would know I wasn't going crazy."

"I think we're both crazy," Janees said. "I need some time to think."

She turned and started to walk away.

"Where are you going?" I asked.

"Where I do my best thinking. I saw a restroom back there around the corner," she said. "I'll be back in a minute."

She kept walking and I sat back down at the table.

For a while, I just stared off into space. It's what I do when I'm trying to figure something out. And, man, did I have some things to figure out...

Just then, a rusty, reddish-orange Ford pickup truck with a cap on the back slowed to a stop at the curb facing the wrong direction. Three men inside the cab looked out the driver's window at me. That kind of creeped me out.

The driver, a biggish man with a gray beard and red face, rolled down his window and leaned out. He looked sort of familiar, but I couldn't quite remember where I had seen him.

"Hey, young fella, can you help us out?" he said.

"We're not from around here and we seem to be lost."

I stood up and walked halfway down to the truck. I looked up and down both sides of the street, but there weren't any trusted adults to help me.

"I'm not from here, either," I said, not coming any closer. "My family is here for a conference. Sorry I can't help you."

The man looked at me and frowned.

"Well, maybe you can help us read this map—the type is so small and our old eyes are having a hard time making out the road names," he said. The tall man next to him handed him a big map. "Won't you lend us your strong young eyes for a minute so we can find our road and get on our way?"

I took a couple of steps closer.

"I don't know…" I said, again looking up and down the street. Where in the heck was Janees?

I took another step closer.

The driver opened his door suddenly. "Get in the truck, kid!"

He grabbed for me, but stumbled to his knees as he got out of the truck and hit the grass.

I turned around and rabbited. I never really understood that expression when I heard a kid use it at school—rabbited. But that's exactly what I did. I kicked off with both feet and ran for my life toward the coffee shop. Just like a rabbit.

The driver got to his feet and made another grab for me. I zigged and he almost fell again.

I yelled, "Help!" but no one was around to hear me.

I was almost back at the coffee shop when the bearded man yelled.

"Get out of the truck and help me, you fools! We need to catch this kid!"

I made it to the doors and yanked at the handle.

Locked! Now what?

The other two men had gotten out of the truck: one tall with a bad scar on the left side of his face and one short with big black eyebrows that almost hid his eyes. They looked familiar, too. But from where? The tall man suddenly had a knife in his hand and seemed to be almost smiling. When the bearded man turned toward them to shout orders, I saw my chance. I hopped over a table that had been chained to a pair of chairs and ran around the building.

I could see the edge of the woods about thirty yards up the hill. If I could just make it to the trees, maybe I could hide until Janees or my uncles came looking for me. I ran.

But before I could get too far, I felt a strong tug at my shoulders that almost yanked me off my feet. The bearded man had taken ahold of my backpack. And the other two men had almost caught up to us.

"Now I've got you, you little urchin," the bearded man said.

I was finished.

As he pulled me toward him, the top of my backpack came open. The leather bundle on top rolled around. The leather flapped open. Then the crystal began to grow a bright blue.

"What the?" the bearded man said. It almost sounded like a yelp.

Whoooomph! Red lightning bolts shot out in all directions, knocking the three men to the ground. They looked stunned. Their arms and legs spread out in odd directions all around them.

I wasn't going to waste my chance. I hitched the backpack up on my shoulders and bolted up the hill.

I made it to the woods before the men regained their senses and got to their feet. They ran up the hill, but their legs seemed wobbly. I ran deeper into the woods. I ran until my chest ached and my legs burned. But I didn't stop. Not until I got to a clearing with a huge log lying on the ground. I jumped over the log and lay down on the other side.

I panted and racked my brain. What the heck could these guys want with me? Like I keep telling everybody, I'm just a kid. No one special. Just a normal, scared kid.

Maybe if I just stayed here, kept my head down, and stayed quiet, I'll be safe. No one would be able to see me in my hiding spot.

"Hello, boy."

My heart jumped out of my chest.

They'd found me!

Finding Bigfoot

Chooch Tenkiller

I got up, ready to run. Then I saw him. He raised a hairy arm with his palm out toward me.

"It's okay, atsutsa. You're safe here."

Tsul'kalu.

I breathed a sigh of relief. Then I almost started to cry.

Almost.

"Wait, how come I can see you without touching the crystal?" I asked him, as if that was the most important question in my crazy life right now.

"Chooch, I can be seen—or unseen—as I choose. The crystal allows you to see more of the world around you, including spirit beings, but only if we choose to be seen," he explained.

I nodded.

"Okay, we need to get out of here. Find someplace to hide—three guys just tried to kidnap me down there," I said, pointing back toward campus.

Tsul'kalu shook his head. "You're in no danger here. They won't find you."

I must have looked skeptical because he went on. "As long as you are with me, you are in no danger. No one will see you unless I allow them to. You are safe, but we need to talk. Come with me."

TIME TO REGROUP

Dr. Almasty and His Henchmen

In the woods near
the university,
Thursday morning

"Where the heck did that little scamp go?" Dottle asked. He panted as he flailed his arms at low branches and bramble bushes.

"How the blazes would I know?" Dr. Almasty snapped. "He was right in front of us and then he wasn't. He must be here somewhere. Keep looking, you fools."

The three men spread out. Nuppence grabbed a long, pointed branch and began to poke it into the thick bushes violently, like a spear.

Dr. Almasty trotted over and grabbed the stick from his hands.

"You idiot! We need the kid alive…for now. He hasn't translated the rock for us yet," Dr. Almasty said. He poked his finger into Nuppence's chest. The taller man stood his ground but leaned his head back, as if he were avoiding an angry chicken or a buzzing hornet.

"All right, all right, keep your shirt on, Almasty," Nuppence said.

"Doctor Almasty! Doctor! How many times do I have to tell you idiots I am a doctor? And you will address me as such."

Dottle snickered. He couldn't help it. He tried to hide his mistake by beating at some nearby bushes and calling out, "Here, kid. Where are you? Hey, kid?"

Dr. Almasty shot a look his way.

"You have something to add, Dottle?"

Dottle looked back at him blankly.

"I don't think he's here, Alm—er, Dr. Almasty," he said. "Maybe we should look for him somewhere else."

Dr. Almasty started to respond but stopped himself. He scratched at his beard.

"You know something, Dottle? You might be right," he said.

Dr. Almasty turned back toward campus.

"Well, come on, come on. What are you two waiting for? Let's get back to the cabin and come up with a new plan."

THE MESSENGER

Chooch Tenkiller

I looked around the large cave. Dim light came in through the opening, which was covered by kudzu vines and small trees. If you've never seen kudzu, count yourself lucky. The thick, green leafy vine grows everywhere in the South, covering trees, buildings— sometimes swallowing whole towns. It's almost like something out of a horror movie. But it's real. And, as I now know, so is Bigfoot.

Tsul'kalu brought in an armload of wood and started a fire in the center of the cavern. It lit the rest of the space where we stood. The top of the cavern was really high. The walls were uneven stone marked by years of smoke. A few large rocks were placed around

97

the cavern. They had all been worn smooth, roughly in the shape of chairs. They reminded me of the big, puffy armchairs in my aunt Pearl's living room, without the big ugly flowers printed on them. Animal hides covered the floor and some of the rock chairs—deer, bear, and some others I didn't recognize. A large metal pot stood against the wall, along with a few large sticks that looked like they were used to poke the fire. The cavern seemed very old and lived-in.

"Is this your home?" I asked Tsul'kalu.

"It's one of the places where I stay," he said. "Sit, Chooch. Let's talk. I know you must have many questions."

I'll say.

We sat on two of the stone chairs that faced each other, with the fire between us.

"Do you know why those men were chasing me?" I asked.

"Not exactly," he said. "But I could probably guess. I believe it has something to do with my rock."

"Well, they can have it. I don't want it."

"I know, Chooch, but it's not that simple," Tsul'kalu said, shaking his head. "Those men think the markings on my rock are a treasure map."

"But they're not!" I said, starting to get up.

"I know, Chooch. And now so do you, thanks to Ulvsati, the crystal," he said, gesturing to my backpack. "It allowed you to see my markings as they were meant to be seen. And it allowed you to hear them when they spoke, didn't it?"

I nodded. "And they danced and sang, too."

He smiled.

"Indeed, they did. They sang a song I taught them long ago. And long before that, when Earth was young, the thunderbirds taught me that song. Did you understand the message?"

"I think so," I said. "But why did they tell me about the dangers facing Earth? And what am I supposed to do about it? I'm just one person. A kid."

Tsul'kalu leaned toward me. His face was serious.

"You are our messenger. We need you to share this message with the world. The Little People and I cannot. People would be afraid of us. They wouldn't listen. But you can bring our message. You'll know when the time is right."

I shook my head. "No one will listen to me."

"Maybe not at first," Tsul'kalu said. "But you need to keep sharing the message. People will understand in time. They must."

He paused. "Do you have any other questions for me?"

"Yes. Why did the Little Person in the woods tell me he knew I was coming? He said they have stories about me. But that's impossible. I'm just a normal kid."

"Awatisgi—the one you met in the woods is named Awatisgi—is the Finder. He knew of you because we have stories about you. And I had a dream about you. We all knew a messenger was coming. You are that messenger, Chooch."

I felt my face start to get hot. I shook my head.

"But why me?" I asked.

"Why? Sometimes our stories don't answer that question. I think you know that, coming from a family of storytellers," Tsul'kalu said. "But I imagine the person who first told this story thought you would be strong enough to meet the challenge. The storyteller knew that you would be brave. That you would still be connected to our culture. That you would believe your eyes and be able to carry our message to the people who needed to hear it."

I thought for a moment. It was true that many of the stories my uncles told focused on the what and the where, but not necessarily the why. Sometimes the listener just had to take it on faith that this is what happened.

I looked up into Tsul'kalu's eyes and gave a slight nod of understanding. Tsul'kalu reached down and gently squeezed my shoulder.

"I know this is a lot to understand," he said. "But it's important. The fate of the whole world really is in your hands. Do you think you can do what I ask?"

I thought about the question. I felt my heartbeat slow to normal and a calm begin to flow over me, almost like water. Maybe he was right. Maybe there was more to life than just being a regular kid, playing sports, and reading comic books. Maybe... I thought of my grandma. My mom. My uncles. Yes.

"Yes," I said. "I am a strong Cherokee person. My family has taught me how to take care of myself and carry out my responsibilities. I can do this!"

"Osdadv! That's great, my son. Now we should get you back to your family so they don't worry."

He led me to the opening of the cave and out into the warm sunlight.

Janees Walks into a Trap

Janees Hollow Horn

Where the heck is Chooch? I haven't been gone that long.

A pickup truck was parked on the wrong side of the road near where Chooch and I had been sitting. Its doors were standing open, but no one was around. The truck was rusty and banged up. I could smell stale cigarette smoke and coffee coming from the cab of the truck. Yuck. Double yuck.

What was the truck doing here? And where in the heck had Chooch run off to? It was almost lunchtime and we needed to get back to the conference center before our uncles came looking for us. Again.

Just then, three men walked around the side of the coffee shop. All three were creepy looking. I didn't want to stick around here with the three of them. But I didn't want to lose Chooch, either.

Maybe he went back to the conference center already. But he wouldn't go back without me, would he?

"Hey, little girl," the creepy old guy with the beard and dark glasses called to me. "Can you help us?"

The creepy tall man with him grinned a fake grin as he tucked something into his belt under his shirt. The creepy short man, who appeared to have a big woolly bear crawling across his creepy forehead, waved a creepy wave at me. Did I mention that all three of them were really creepy? Well, they were, and weirdly familiar. They must have been on our hike or at the bonfire last night.

I took a step back, but I didn't say anything. My mom had taught me to always have an escape route. My best escape route seemed to be down the sidewalk toward the conference center or around the side of the coffee shop, up the hill, and into the woods. I thought about both in a split second. The sidewalk escape route was straight and direct. But I'm not a fast runner and the three men would probably catch me. I am a good hider, though. If I could make it to the woods, I bet I could find a hiding place and stay out of sight until they left.

"Little girl," the bearded man said again.

I didn't answer. I just turned and started walking toward the coffee shop.

"Get her, you fools," the bearded man yelled. "Grab her and get her in the truck! Do whatever you have to do, but get her."

My insides grew cold and my heart started beating in my ears. I felt tears start to form in the corner of my eyes. I couldn't let these guys catch me.

I started to run. Like I said, I'm not fast, but I didn't have too far to go.

I ran back toward the coffee shop. I could hear heavy footsteps behind me as the three creepy men chased me. As I rounded the corner of the building, I slipped on the grass and fell down hard. I pushed myself up and was just about to my feet when I felt myself lifted off the ground by a pair of large hands grabbing my sweatshirt.

"Gotcha!" the bearded man said. I could feel his hot breath on my neck as he set me down and spun me around. I started to whimper. I couldn't help it. My eyes were filling with tears and my stomach was tied up in knots. What were they going to do to me?

Just when the fear and panic were about to get the best of me, I remembered the other piece of advice my mother had given me: Fight back. Scratch, claw, punch, or kick!

I looked up into the tinted eyeglasses and bearded face of my captor, and I kicked him as hard as I could right between the legs.

"*Ding!* Give the girl a prize!" I said, remembering another lesson my mom had taught me: use humor when scared or sad. It's a way the Cherokee cope with overwhelming situations.

The bearded man's face went blank; he obviously didn't see the humor in the situation. Then he turned an ugly shade of green. Without making a sound, the bearded man fell to the ground and curled up into a ball.

I didn't waste a second. I spun on my heels and ran back up the hill. Without slowing down, I burst through the bushes into the woods.

I ran through the forest as fast as I could go. Branches tore at my blouse and scratched my face and arms. But I didn't care. I had to keep going. The farther I ran into the woods, the safer I would be.

Where was Chooch? I could use some help here.

I ran into a clearing with a small stream running through it. A large stump, bigger than I was, stood along the banks of the creek. Wild grapes and brambles lined the edges of the clearing. The spot was beautiful, but I didn't have time to listen to the birds and smell the flowers. I was in danger!

I sat down on the other side of the stump and leaned back against the rough bark. My chest hurt from breathing so hard.

As my breathing settled down, I started to cry. I was scared and alone in the woods. Men were chasing me. My cousin was lost. But then I got angry. I'm stronger than they think. I'm smart and I can figure out a way to get out of this mess. I nodded my head once, even though there was no one there to see me.

Or so I thought.

"Janees! What are you doing here?"

It was Chooch. The one who had wandered off and abandoned me to human traffickers or whoever those creepy guys are.

"Chooch," I said as I ran over to him and hugged him. "We have to get out of here. These bad guys tried to kidnap me and sell me into slavery or something. I barely got away by running into these woods. Wait— what are you doing here?"

Chooch released me from his bear hug. "Were there three of them? A guy with a beard, a tall guy, and a short guy?"

"You saw them?" I asked.

"They chased me, too. I ran into the woods to get away. That's where he found me and helped me get away," Chooch said, pointing to the trees behind him.

"Who?" I asked.

"Him," he said, pointing at the same trees.

I stared at the trees, but I couldn't see anyone.

"She can't see me, Chooch," said a deep, rumbling voice coming out of thin air near my cousin. "Hand her Ulvsati."

I stepped back. "What the heck is that? Are you some sort of ventriloquist all of a sudden?"

Chooch took his backpack off and opened the top. He pulled out the shiny rock he'd handed me earlier. I shook my head no and took another step back.

"Here, Janees, trust me. Take the crystal. There's someone I want you to meet."

Chooch walked over, gently lifted my right arm, and put the crystal in my hand. Sparks flew. I felt dizzy. Everything around me seemed to be covered with a blue haze. Then I saw him. It. Him? Bigfoot. A giant, hairy Bigfoot. Right here with us. And he talked!

"Cuz, this is Tsul'kalu. He saved me when those men were chasing me. He's our friend."

My mouth stayed open. I couldn't speak, my throat had closed up, and my mouth was dry. I started to shake my head again.

"Osiyo, Janees. Tsul'kalu daquadoa," the large hairy man said, raising his right hand, which was bigger than my whole head. "They call me Tsul'kalu, Janees. I'm glad to meet you."

Chooch just looked at me and grinned.

"See, I told you."

WILL ANYONE BELIEVE US?

Chooch Tenkiller

Back on campus,
Thursday afternoon

"We have to get back to the conference center," I told Janees as we peered around the corner of the coffee shop.

"Yeah, but we'll never make it if those human traffickers grab us," she said.

"Treasure hunters," I corrected her.

"What?"

"They're treasure hunters. They think Judaculla Rock is some kind of treasure map. And for some reason, they think I can help them find their treasure."

"But why grab me?" she asked.

Good question.

"Maybe they knew we were related?"

"How?" she asked.

"Maybe they just figured, 'What are the odds?' I mean they saw two Indian kids hanging out on a college campus in the summer and put two and two together? I don't know."

The truck was gone and the sidewalks on both sides of the street looked deserted. Janees and I walked slowly down the hill and turned toward the conference center.

"We'd better get back and tell our uncles about these guys," she said. "They'll know what to do. We should call the cops."

I didn't answer. I wondered what we would tell our uncles. I couldn't tell them about Tsul'kalu, the Little People, or the crystal. Even though our uncles believed in all this stuff and told stories about spirit beings, I just didn't think they'd believe I had actually seen them.

When we got back to the conference center, we found our uncles and told them about the strange guys chasing us.

"Are you okay? Did they hurt you?" Uncle Jack asked as he hugged Janees tightly to him.

"Where are the men now? Did you see where they went?" Uncle Dynamite asked me. The look on his face was dark. I had never seen him so angry.

"No, Unc. They were gone when Janees and I came out of the woods. We hid for a long time before we walked out of the trees to look," I said. "We're okay. Just shaken up."

"Yes, we're okay now. Now that we're back with you," Janees said as she buried her face into Uncle Jack's chest.

Uncle Jack squeezed his niece's arm reassuringly.

"We should call the police," he said. "Maybe they can find those guys and take them to jail."

"Are you sure we should call the police? We're fine now. And I don't really want to be questioned all afternoon by a police officer," I said.

"We should call them." Uncle Dynamite agreed with his brother. "We would feel awful if those guys grabbed another kid and did something terrible."

I nodded.

"I guess you're right," I said.

Janees released Uncle Jack and turned toward us.

"Of course they're right," she said. "Those guys tried to grab two different kids off the street—you and me, Chooch—just minutes apart. They could try again. They probably will."

When the police officer arrived, we all went into a seating area away from the conference. There were eight big chairs arranged around a glass coffee table. We all sat down and looked at the police officer. His name was Lopez, according to his badge. He looked like he might be Cherokee, but I wasn't sure. He had a tablet computer and a gray computer pen that he used for taking notes.

"Maurice and Janees, tell me what happened from the beginning. Why don't you start, Maurice?" Officer Lopez said.

I told him about the three men and their pickup truck. I told him about their attempt to grab me. I described the three men as best I could remember, which wasn't much. But I didn't tell Officer Lopez how I really got away or about Tsul'kalu. He wouldn't have believed me, even if I did tell him.

Janees told her story, leaving out the same things I did.

When we finished, Officer Lopez said, "Is there anything else either of you remember about the men? We don't have much to go on."

Janees and I shook our heads.

"All right then," he said, standing up. "We'll put out the descriptions on the radio and the details about the truck. Officers will be on the lookout. Not much more we can do at this time."

As he walked toward the doors, he beckoned to Uncle Jack and Uncle Dynamite. They walked over to the officer while Janees and I stayed in our seats.

We could hear the adults talking in low voices. I guess they thought we couldn't hear them. But we could.

"Gentlemen, we see a few cases like this every year. Kids claim that someone tried to grab them off the street, but those real cases are so rare. Most of the time, we find out that the kids just had very active imaginations," Officer Lopez said. "We'll keep an eye out for this rusty red pickup truck, but that's about as far as this will go. I'd suggest you keep a closer eye on your children and talk with them about why it's important to always tell the truth to the police."

I could tell from the way my uncles were standing and holding their heads that they were angry.

"Officer Lopez, my niece and nephew aren't the type of kids to make up stories or waste the police department's time," Uncle Dynamite said.

I looked over at Janees and she was grinning.

"If they say three men tried to kidnap them," Uncle Jack said, "then three men tried to kidnap them. And the police should do everything they can to find those dangerous men and arrest them."

Officer Lopez took a half step back.

"I don't mean to upset you," he said. "But I'm telling you what my experience has been with this type of case. Y'all have a nice evening. And stay safe."

After Officer Lopez left, our uncles walked back over to us.

"I guess you heard some of that claptrap," Uncle Jack said.

Janees and I nodded.

"You know that we believe you both, right?" Uncle Dynamite said.

We nodded again.

"And we'll do whatever it takes to keep you safe," he added.

Uncle Jack extended a hand and helped Janees up from her comfy chair. "Come on, you two," he said. "We're going back to our rooms to pack up our stuff. I don't want to stay here one more night while those bad guys are on the loose."

Uncle Dynamite held the door for us.

"Besides, we're taking the long way back," he said. "There's a stop your uncle and I want to make on our way home. It's someplace we've always wanted to visit, so we can't pass up the chance."

"What is it? Where are we stopping?" I asked.

"Either of you ever heard of the Mothman?" Uncle Jack asked.

THE MOTHMAN

Chooch Tenkiller

"What the heck is a moth man?" I asked as our car headed up the highway. "Is it like a wolf man, but with bugs?"

"Maybe it's like in that movie, *The Fly*," Janees said. "You know, that gross movie where that guy turned into a giant slobbering fly?"

Uncle Jack and Uncle Dynamite both laughed.

"Well, something like that," Uncle Jack said. "You want to tell this one, brother?"

"Hawa, I've got it," Uncle Dynamite said. He turned around in his seat and looked at Janees and me. His face grew serious.

"Ilvhiyu tsigesv—a long time ago—the Cherokee people lived all over this part of the world," he started.

Janees and I settled into our seats, prepared for a long story.

"But we weren't the only ones who lived here. There were the four-leggeds, the birds, the fish, and the spirit beings. There were the Muscogee, the Catawba, and other Indian people. And, there was another group of people. They were different. Very different."

He paused as if anticipating a question.

Janees and I stared at Uncle Dynamite, but I didn't want to disappoint him, so I finally asked, "What do you mean 'different'?"

Uncle Dynamite's face lit up with a satisfied smile before he went on with his story:

"These people were tall. Very tall. Not as tall as someone like Tsul'kalu, but taller than the tallest Cherokee person. They were also white. And when I say 'white,' I don't mean white like the non-Indian people who came here from Europe.

"They were white like snow. White like an egret feather. Pale. Almost see-through. And they were kind of like cars, right, Jack?"

Uncle Dynamite laughed and Uncle Jack gave him a "get out of here" gesture with his right hand, while keeping his eyes on the road.

"He's making a joke about our word for 'car,'" Uncle Jack explained, without really clearing anything up, at least for me.

I looked at Janees and she shrugged.

"Digatuleni is one of our words for 'car,'" Uncle Dynamite said, still chuckling. "That word literally means 'it has big eyes' because a car has those big headlights in front."

"So these white people had big eyes that were pure black. These tall, white people lived in their own villages in the hills near us. We all knew they were there, but we let them be and we never went to their towns. And they never came to ours.

"But they say that one day the Cherokee and these tall, white people went to war. No one remembers why. But when we fought, the white people revealed that they had giant wings. They could fly. We had never seen anything like that before.

"The Cherokee drove the winged white people out. Some say the winged ones moved east. And we didn't think of them again for many, many years until people started seeing this Mothman. The elders say he is one of the winged white people. Others say he is some sort of spaceman or alien. But I don't believe in that sort of thing."

So aliens are fake, but my uncle believes in Little People and Bigfoot. Right.

Oh, wait, so do I.

"They built a museum dedicated to the Mothman up there in West Virginia, where we're headed. It's near a place where people saw this Mothman many years ago. The museum is supposed to have recordings of witness statements and drawings of the creature. Your uncle and I want to check it out and see if this Mothman is one of our winged snow-white people. It's worth a look. Plus, I hear they have a great gift shop. Maybe we can get your moms something," Uncle Dynamite said. "So settle in. We won't be there for several more hours—after midnight. We'll stay in a motel nearby and hit the museum first thing in the morning."

My eyes had already started to grow heavy. I leaned back into my seat and let the bouncing of the car rock me to sleep.

I woke up when Janees patted me on the leg.

"Hey, cuz, we're at the motel. Let's go in and sleep in a real bed even if we have to share. This sleeping in a car is not fun. Plus, it's killing my back and neck."

We stumbled into the motel room and flopped down on the beds. Janees was asleep before my uncles turned out the light.

21

PREDATORS

Dr. Almasty and His Henchmen

The pickup pulled into the motel parking lot and drove slowly past the parked cars. The three men inside the cramped, warm cab craned their necks as they scanned the lot.

"There it is," Dr. Almasty said. "That ugly station wagon is hard to miss."

Dr. Almasty drove a couple rows over and parked facing the car. All three men sat and stared at the car. The silence dragged on for several minutes.

"Do we grab him now?" Dottle asked, breaking the spell.

"No, you idiot. We wait until morning and see what they're up to," Dr. Almasty said. "Wherever they go, we go. And when the opportunity presents itself, we snatch the kid."

Dottle nodded. Nuppence snored softly on the other side of the cab.

Nuppence had an amazing capacity for drifting off to sleep whenever the opportunity presented itself.

"Nuppence is already asleep. I'm going to get some shut-eye, too. So you take the first watch," Dr. Almasty said. "Do not fall asleep. You watch that car and wake us if that kid shows up. It's almost one. Wake me at three and I'll take the next shift."

HOME OF THE MOTHMAN

Chooch Tenkiller

Mothman Museum,
Point Pleasant, West Virginia,
Friday morning

"Now that was a good breakfast," Uncle Jack said as we walked out of the motel and into the parking lot. "Grits, scrambled eggs, and bacon—the three food groups."

"You forgot coffee," Uncle Dynamite said before taking a sip of his coffee from a foam take-out cup. "And some biscuits and sausage gravy would have rounded things out. There are five food groups, brother."

"Yeah, but Chooch and I were really embarrassed by what you did in there, Uncle Jack," Janees said.

Uncle Jack stopped on the sidewalk and tilted

his head at Janees. "What?" he asked. "How did I embarrass you?"

He seemed genuinely concerned and equally clueless.

Janees stared right back at him, one hand planted firmly on her hip. You know, the "mom is really mad" stance.

"Honestly, you don't know what you did? Help me out here, Chooch," Janees said.

"She's talking about when you dropped your bacon on the floor," I said, trying to help him remember.

"What about it?" Uncle Jack said. "I didn't leave it there. I picked it up."

"And then you ate it!" Janees said. "You ate it. Eww."

Uncle Jack had the same blank look on his face that he gets when he tries to open an email attachment, complete with one raised eyebrow. He looked over to Uncle Dynamite, who just shook his head and shrugged.

"Haven't you ever heard of the three-second rule, Unc?" I asked.

"Kids," Uncle Jack said. "When you get to be an elder like me and your uncle Dynamite, there's no such thing as a three-second rule. We have a thirty-second rule. Takes us that long to bend down and straighten back up."

"Hawa," Uncle Dynamite said. Then they both started to laugh.

When they looked back at me and Janees, they both frowned. My cuz's face looked a tad greenish.

"You feeling okay?" Uncle Dynamite asked Janees.

Janees nodded her head, but her face clearly signaled "no."

"How far is the museum?" Janees asked, holding her belly and beginning to sweat. That fourth large blueberry pancake might have been a mistake.

"It's not too far. It opens at ten, so we'll get there just as they're turning the lights on," Uncle Dynamite said. "Sure you're okay, Wesa?"

Janees nodded her head again but didn't say a word.

We drove out of the parking lot and headed down the road. It was going to be a long day.

At the time, I had no idea how long.

But I soon found out. And not in a good way.

We parked our car in the lot just down the street from the museum. The museum looked like an old store with a blue-and-white-striped awning along its front. It cost $18 for the four of us to go inside. My uncles could have saved $9 by letting Janees and me wait outside, but they insisted we go in with them. I think they were a little nervous after what happened at the college yesterday.

"Holay! Look at this place," Uncle Dynamite said as we entered the large main room of the museum, crammed full of life-size Mothman models, photos, and other odd items related to the monster that had made this town famous. Sort of.

Janees ran over to a mannequin wearing a black suit, white shirt, and thin black tie. The mannequin also wore a dark hat and sunglasses, like some federal agent in an old movie.

"Hey, Chooch, take my photo with Slender Man," Janees said.

I pulled out my phone and took her picture. She stuck out her tongue and rolled her eyes. So you could definitely say I captured her best side.

She was obviously feeling better. Her pancake sweats seemed to have passed. That would make our car ride a little easier after we finally got out of this boring museum.

My uncles wandered over to a big glass case with old newspapers and yellowed photos.

"Nothing in here about the Mothmen battling the Cherokee people," Uncle Jack said to his brother.

"Did you really think the newspapers around here

would include our stories?" Uncle Dynamite snorted. "As if. That's why you and I have to keep on telling them. Someone has to keep the truth alive and pass it on to the next generation."

"That's so," Uncle Jack agreed.

My uncles moved on to the next case while Janees and I explored the museum, peeking behind displays and trying to find secret rooms and hidden passages.

"It shouldn't be much longer," I reassured Janees. "We still have a long drive ahead and I know Uncle Jack will be getting hungry again soon."

"Oof," Janees said. "Don't mention food or I'll be carsick for the next sixteen hours."

"Thirteen," I said.

"What?" Janees asked.

"We have only thirteen more hours to go in the car," I said. "Plus, I think our uncles are planning to stop for the night in Chicago. That'll break up the ride."

Janees just scowled at me and shook her head.

STEALTHY STALKERS

Dr. Almasty and His Henchmen

Inside the Mothman Museum,
Friday morning

The tall, mustachioed man stepped out from behind a large wooden Mothman Museum display and began to follow the Indian boy with the long braid and the girl with him. He kept his distance and stopped to look at one of the display cases anytime the boy or the girl turned to look his way.

A second man, gray-bearded, dressed for cold weather on one of the hottest days of the summer, stared at the boy and girl from across the room. He leaned against a wall and kept pulling his large hat down over his eyes and adjusting the popped collar on his baggy trench coat as if to keep out a cold rain.

The second man stepped away from the wall and began to walk a big circle around the kids as if stalking them. He gradually made his way around them and slid between two displays to lie in wait.

"What are you doing? Peeping at those young people?" A mother with a small child over her shoulder and another hanging on to her leg angrily confronted the bearded man in the trench coat.

"Do you work here? Are you an actor or something?" she asked with a note of suspicion in her voice, as if she already knew the answer. "Or should I go alert the staff to a case of stranger danger?" She asked the last bit in a much louder voice. The child over her shoulder woke from his nap and started to cry. It sounded like rockets going off.

"Lady, mind your own business," the man snarled, backing farther down the aisle.

Chooch and Janees stopped and stared at the two adults arguing. The tall man who had been following them ducked behind another display and began his escape.

Before the woman could haul him to the manager to answer for his weird behavior, the bearded man turned and walked away quickly, cutting between two glass cases and making a dash for the front entrance.

As he rounded another group of displays, he slammed into the back of the tall man.

"Out of my way, you fool!" squealed the bearded man. "We mustn't get caught!"

The two odd men ran through the gift shop and out the door into the summer heat.

24

PLAN B—OR IS IT C?

Dr. Almasty and His Henchmen

Outside the Mothman Museum,
Friday morning

Dr. Almasty and Nuppence climbed back into the truck, which was parked across the street from the museum, and slammed their doors. Nuppence ripped off his fake mustache and pulled off his knit cap. Dr. Almasty shrugged off the large floppy hat and baggy trench coat. They both looked angrily at Dottle.

"What?" Dottle asked.

"We couldn't get to the kid. That place is too crowded with junk and there were people all over," Nuppence said. "The World's Only Mothman Museum. Yeah, right. Like someone would be dumb enough to build another one."

Dr. Almasty gripped the steering wheel so tightly that the knuckles of his red hands turned a yellowish white. "We're going to have to follow them some more. We can make the grab the next time they stop at a gas station or a rest area. Someplace less crowded," he said. "We just need to find a way to get him away from the other people traveling with him."

Dottle squirmed in his seat. It wasn't exactly comfortable between Dr. Almasty and Nuppence.

"Quit your wiggling around, you fool," Dr. Almasty said. "You're not a jumping bean. Sit still."

"We drove for seven hours last night and then slept in this stupid truck," Dottle snarled. "I'm tired of being cooped up in here, squashed between you two."

He raised his arms in an exaggerated stretch. At the same time, Nuppence and Dr. Almasty each drove an elbow into Dottle's ribs.

"Hey! That hurts, you guys!" he said.

"Good," Dr. Almasty and Nuppence said at the same time.

Dr. Almasty reached up and turned the key in the ignition. The old truck coughed to life. It shook as it warmed up.

Dr. Almasty cracked his window a bit, then reached

up to grab his binoculars off the dashboard. He trained them on the front of the museum.

"We don't want to lose them now. I'll watch the door. You keep an eye on their car in the parking lot, Nuppence, in case they slip out a side exit."

"Okay," the tall man said.

They sat like that for more than an hour. The inside of the truck was like an oven. Dottle began to cook in his own sweat. Or at least it felt like he was cooking.

But he wasn't going to say anything. They just needed to wait a while longer, grab the kid when the chance presented itself, and hightail it to the treasure map—a treasure map that just looked like a big rock to him, but he wasn't the doctor, now was he? He'd have to trust Dr. Almasty and ride it out for the big payday that was just around the corner.

"There they are!" Dr. Almasty said. "They're heading to their car. Get ready, me boys. We're about to go on a chase."

They followed the orange station wagon up Highway 35 for a half hour before it put on its blinker and drifted toward the exit. The car pulled into a truck stop and parked at the gas pumps. Dr. Almasty pulled his truck into a parking space nearby and watched.

The two elderly Indian men got out of the car and

stretched. They made a lot of groaning and creaking sounds.

"I have to use the little boys' room," the chubby one said to the taller Indian guy.

"Me, too," said the tall one. "Let's get the gas started and Chooch can watch the pump for us."

He leaned in the car and talked to the two kids. Both got out. The little girl was going in the truck stop with the two older guys! Finally, a break!

The kid stood on the left side of the station wagon, looking at his phone and not really paying attention to the pump.

"Now, gentlemen," Dr. Almasty said. "Now is our chance to grab the little urchin and get away before the old guys and the girl get back. But we have to move fast."

The three men stepped out of the truck. Dottle could barely straighten his spine. And his legs wobbled.

"Dottle, open that back hatch of the cab and get ready to shove the kid in when we grab him," Dr. Almasty said in a loud whisper. "Nuppence. You loop around the front of the car in case he gets away from me or makes a break for it."

"Roger that," Nuppence said, as he drew his knife

from its sheath. "And if I have to cut him a little to make him see reason, all the better."

"Fine, just don't kill him," Dr. Almasty said. "Yet."

The two kidnappers began to stalk the boy like a pair of jackals. They circled their prey, trying to stay out of his line of sight for as long as possible. Dr. Almasty swept his eyes around the parking lot, making sure there were no witnesses or anyone who might try to help the kid.

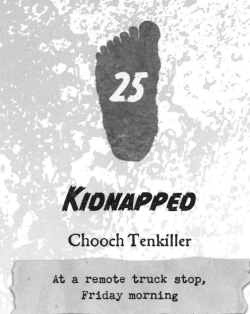

KIDNAPPED

Chooch Tenkiller

At a remote truck stop,
Friday morning

I tucked my phone into my jeans pocket and looked up at the numbers rolling by on the gas pump. How much gas did this car hold, anyway? My stomach growled. With any luck, my uncles would grab me some trail mix or a bag of pretzels.

Wham!

I had no idea what hit me. My world started to spin and I felt something—someone—grabbing me.

"Mmmmf!" I tried to yell as a large red hand clamped down over my mouth.

I felt myself being dragged backward. Then I saw a

familiar-looking tall man running toward me. It was one of the kidnappers from yesterday. They'd found us! What in the heck did they want? Why wouldn't they leave us alone? And how in the world had they found us in the middle of West Virginia?

The men pulled me to the back of their pickup, where the third man was waiting with an old sack in his hand. He put the sack over my head, so the whole world grew dark. I started to scream when I felt a sharp pain in the side of my neck, and then...

Nothing.

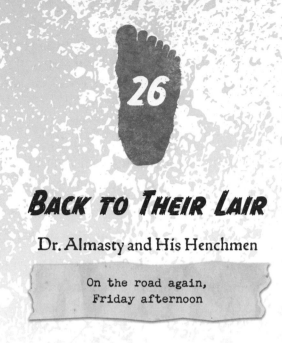

Back to Their Lair

Dr. Almasty and His Henchmen

On the road again,
Friday afternoon

The three men rode silently as the truck sped down the highway back toward their hideout in North Carolina. The kid was out cold in the back of the truck, thanks to the shot that Dr. Almasty had given him at the truck stop.

Dottle thought that would be a terrible way to ride—tied up, with a bag over your head, and rolling around in the back of a dirty pickup truck. Good thing it was that kid and not him. He got a shiver.

"The kid should be out for at least eight or nine hours," Dr. Almasty said as he drove. "The drive back to the cabin will take us only six or seven. We shouldn't have any issues with the kid. But we'll stop and check on him every couple of hours. I'll give him another dose of sedative if he stirs."

Dr. Almasty's mood suddenly brightened.

"And at first light tomorrow, we'll drag his skinny body out to that rock and make him read that treasure map for us," he said.

"Right, boss," Dottle said. "Your plan worked."

"Well, of course it worked, you idiot," Dr. Almasty snapped. "I am the brains of this outfit."

"What kind of doctor are you anyway?" Nuppence asked. "Kid doctor? Surgeon? What?"

Dr. Almasty reddened.

"I am an anthropologist," he said. "With a Ph.D. That kind of doctor."

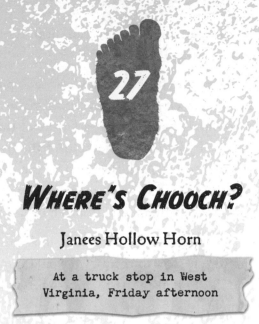

WHERE'S CHOOCH?

Janees Hollow Horn

At a truck stop in West
Virginia, Friday afternoon

"Now where did our nephew run off to? Did you see him inside?" Uncle Jack gestured toward the car sitting at the gas pump. The gas nozzle was still in the tank. But Chooch was nowhere to be found. Good thing those gas pumps shut off by themselves when the car is full.

"Chooch? Hadlv? Where are you?" Uncle Dynamite called out, but there was no one around to hear him. Chooch must have gone inside the truck stop to use the restroom or to find a snack, I thought.

"You two stay here. I'll go back inside and find that

boy so we can get back on the road. Still a long trip ahead of us," Uncle Dynamite said.

I crawled into the back seat as Uncle Jack put back the gas nozzle and closed the gas cap. It made a *click-click-click* sound as he twisted it a few extra turns for good measure. I listened to the hum of the overhead lights and watched fat black flies circling the trash can between the pumps. The smell of gasoline was thick, almost unbearable. It made my stomach queasy again.

Uncle Jack opened his door and took his place behind the wheel. "I wish those two would hurry up," he said. "I'd like to make it past Chicago before we pull in for the night."

I looked around the car. Then I saw it: Chooch's backpack.

"He wouldn't have gone anywhere without his backpack," I said, pointing to the bag. "That's where he keeps his money. If he went in for a snack, he would have definitely taken his bag."

Uncle Jack thought about that, then turned back around in his seat to watch for his brother and nephew. The door to the convenience store opened and Uncle Dynamite walked out. Alone.

"Oh no," Uncle Jack said. "Something is wrong. Where's our nephew?"

"I couldn't find him," Uncle Dynamite said as he opened his car door and leaned in. "And no one inside has seen a tall Indian boy. I don't want to worry, but it's not like Chooch to disappear like this. He's very responsible."

"Have a seat, brother, and let's give him a few minutes," Uncle Jack said. "I'm sure he'll be out soon. You probably just missed him when you were inside."

I wasn't so sure about that. What if something had happened to Chooch? He could be annoying, but I really do love my cousin. He is like the big brother I never had.

My uncles must have noticed the worry on my face.

"It's okay, Wesa. Your cousin will show up in just a minute," Uncle Jack said. Uncle Jack usually calls me Wesa when he wants to calm me down or make me feel better. That scared me even more.

"What if the kidnappers got him?" I blurted.

Both of my uncles smiled.

"Don't laugh at me," I said. "I'm serious. What if the kidnappers followed us and snatched Chooch when we weren't looking?"

"No one snatched Chooch," Uncle Dynamite said, reaching back and patting my knee reassuringly. "Those bad guys are hundreds of miles away. Probably sitting in a jail cell back there in North Carolina. Besides, they have no reason to follow us up here and grab Chooch. It's not like they have some sort of grudge or something. I mean, what did he ever do to them? Right?"

Uncle Dynamite said that last bit as a way to convince me that Chooch was no longer in danger. But it just made me think of all the reasons the kidnappers might have for following us and grabbing Chooch.

Tears began to run down my cheeks.

"I think the kidnappers grabbed Chooch," I said. "I think I know where they took him. And I think I know why."

I sniffled.

"There's something we haven't told you," I continued.

Both of my uncles turned in their seats and looked at me with wide eyes.

"It's about Tsul'kalu."

JANEES COMES CLEAN

Janees Hollow Horn

Speeding down the highway,
Friday afternoon

I told my uncles the whole story, starting with the Little Person who talked with Chooch in the woods.

They looked at each other and nodded. Not the reaction I was expecting.

I told them about seeing Tsul'kalu in the forest after the kidnappers tried to snatch us in front of the coffee shop. My uncles didn't even blink. Hmmmm.

Then I told them Chooch could read the markings on Judaculla Rock.

And, believe it or not, that's the part they couldn't

believe. Honestly! Like I would make something like that up.

So I opened Chooch's bag (if you're reading this, cuz, I did it only to prove the story to our uncles. I didn't touch anything in your precious backpack besides the crystal. And I didn't really touch that; I just unfolded the old leather bundle enough to show our uncles the crystal inside).

I held out the crystal. It glowed a faint blue and I think it was humming. Weird. I don't remember hearing that before.

"Holay!" Uncle Jack said. "They found Uktena's crystal. I've never seen one before, but Grandpa used to tell us stories about them. Remember? He said he knew a family who was responsible for taking care of one. They had to feed it and keep it hidden. Feed it animal blood."

"Well, I'll be," Uncle Dynamite said. "You should put that away, Janees. Carefully. That's a very powerful object."

I nodded. "I'll say. I touched it back at the college and all of a sudden, I was surrounded by dozens of Little People. Then I got all dizzy and almost fainted."

My uncles nodded slowly. They knew what this crystal was capable of.

I folded the bundle and put it back in Chooch's bag. I buckled the top.

"The kidnappers know that Chooch can read the rock," I continued with my story. "And they think it's some kind of treasure map. But Chooch says it isn't. It's some sort of message to us from the spirit beings who are drawn on the rock."

My uncles both nodded again. They sure were doing a lot of nodding. I couldn't believe how easily they were believing my story. Most of it, anyway.

"I think the kidnappers are taking Chooch back to Judaculla Rock so he can read the markings for them," I said. "We'd better go after them. And fast. He can't read the rock without this crystal. And if he can't read the rock, they won't need him anymore. He's in real danger."

I started to cry again. This was all my fault. I should have told our uncles everything as soon as it happened back at the college. Now Chooch was in danger and I was to blame. I would never forgive myself if something happened to him.

"We'll head back in just a minute," Uncle Dynamite said. "I want to run inside and talk to the truck stop manager. I'll leave Chooch a note and tell him to call my cell phone in case he shows up. I'll leave some money with the manager for Chooch so he can get something to eat while he waits. In case we're wrong—but I think you're right, Wesa."

Uncle Jack looked up at his brother. "Do you think we should call the police?" he asked.

"No. The last time they didn't believe us. And we didn't even mention Little People, Bigfoot, and a magic crystal," Uncle Dynamite said. "Can you imagine what these West Virginia police officers would say when they heard that?"

He got out of the car.

"I'll be right back," he said. "Then we'll go get our nephew back. Heaven help those kidnappers when I get my hands on them."

Dr. Almasty's Daydream

Dr. Almasty and His Henchmen

Heading back to North Carolina,
Friday afternoon

"The kid's still out cold," Nuppence said as he hopped back in the passenger side of the truck. "Too bad. I thought we could have some fun, the kid, my knife, and me."

"Patience, Nuppence," Dr. Almasty said. "We need him alive until he reads the map for us."

The kidnappers had pulled into a rest area near Asheville. They were getting close to their hideout.

It would be good to get some rest back at the cabin and make a plan for the next day. The treasure was almost in their grasp. They just needed the kid to work his magic and read them the map. Then it would be a simple matter to find the loot and grab all the gold they could carry.

The big score Dr. Almasty had been dreaming of since he was a boy was finally here. And he could almost taste it.

The first thing he would do, after his crooked ex-brother-in-law saw to it, would be to buy Judaculla Rock. Then he would blow that boulder to smithereens with some dynamite. After that, he would hire battalions of miners to swarm the hillside, digging tunnels and hauling out carts of ore. He would grow richer by the minute! When he was finished, there would be nothing left of that hill but rubble and one huge pile of cash.

Dr. Almasty shook his head to clear the daydream.

"Let's get back on the road. I want to get to the cabin and lock this kid safely in the cellar. Then I'll finally be able to relax," Dr. Almasty said. "Until then, keep your eyes open and your mouths closed."

The truck pulled back onto the highway. They hadn't seen another car for what seemed like hours. They had the road to themselves.

Except for the burnt-orange station wagon thirty miles behind and gaining on them.

Back at the Hideout

Dr. Almasty and His Henchmen

In a cabin in the
Balsam Mountains,
Friday, late afternoon

It was late in the day when the pickup turned into the almost-hidden driveway deep in the woods near Cullowhee. They had driven straight through, stopping only for gas and to check on the kid. They still hadn't eaten, and Dottle's stomach was really angry now. It growled and moaned every time the truck bumped or bounced on a rut in the road.

Growlllllll. There it was again.

Nuppence and Dr. Almasty both turned to scowl at him.

"Shut up, Dottle," they both said.

The truck made its way through the thick forest, the rough road lined on both sides by balsam and spruce trees. The undergrowth of rhododendron, azaleas, and mountain laurel was so thick that even rabbits and squirrels had a hard time making their way through.

Finally, the truck lurched to a stop outside a tired, brown cabin with a slanted roof and crumbling chimney. Moss and huge cobwebs decorated the front porch, which was missing a few boards.

The three men quickly hopped out of the truck and peeked in at the boy, who was still unconscious.

They went inside the cabin and moved an old sofa to reveal a trapdoor. The sofa's wooden feet screeched as it was dragged across the pine floor planks. Dr. Almasty raised the door, which creaked on rusty hinges. A blast of dank, musty air rose from the open trapdoor and made Dr. Almasty take a small step back. He turned and walked over to the kitchen counter, where he grabbed a flashlight. He returned to the trapdoor and walked down rickety wooden stairs into the damp root cellar. Dr. Almasty waved his left arm and sputtered as he walked through decades of spiderwebs.

"This should be comfortable enough for our young visitor," he said. "He won't be with us for too long. Just until he has made himself useful."

Dottle and Nuppence leaned over the trapdoor and

watched Dr. Almasty survey the small space.

"I didn't think you would really hurt the kid," Dottle said.

Dr. Almasty looked back up the stairs and shined his light in Dottle's eyes.

"That's right, Dottle, that's right," Dr. Almasty said. "We won't hurt him. We'll make it quick. He won't feel a thing."

Nuppence laughed a deep laugh. "Not too quick, though. You promised."

Dottle looked at his feet and gulped. He hadn't signed on for this. He might be a con man and a thief, but he was no murderer. Yet he couldn't very well back out now, not when they were this close. He'd have to think of something.

The three men went out to the truck. Dottle and Nuppence grabbed the boy from the back of the truck. Dottle grabbed the kid under his arms and Nuppence held him by the legs as they carried him inside.

"He's heavier than he looks," Dottle grunted.

"Just shut up and carry your end," Nuppence said, breathing heavily and carefully walking backward toward the cabin.

When they carried Chooch up the front steps, Dottle and Nuppence staggered inside the cabin and over to the trapdoor. Nuppence swung the boy's legs, ready to throw him down the stairs into the cellar.

"Not like that, you fool. Carry him down," Dr. Almasty said. "We need him alive so he can read that map for us."

Nuppence and Dottle carried the boy down to the cellar and laid him on the dirt floor. Weak light filtered in through a small, dirty window high on the far wall. The two henchmen walked back up the stairs and started to close the trapdoor.

"Wait!" Dr. Almasty said, holding up a hand. "We don't want to just leave him down there to roam free when he wakes up."

Dr. Almasty grabbed a coil of rope from a corner of the cabin. He walked over near the chimney and yanked a canvas feed sack off the wall where it had been tacked to hide several large holes in the plaster. He walked back down the stairs. He bent down and grabbed the unconscious boy under his arms and propped him up in an old wooden chair. He tied the boy's ankles and wrists with the rope. Dr. Almasty reached into his pants pocket and pulled out an old bandanna, which he used to gag the boy. Then he pulled the feed sack down over the boy's head.

"There," he said, patting the boy on the top of his

head. "All snug in your bed for the night. Don't let the spiders bite."

Dr. Almasty chuckled as he trudged back up the stairs.

"Here, Nuppence, give me a hand with this," Dr. Almasty said, gesturing to the sofa.

He and Nuppence pushed the sofa back into place, hiding the door in the cabin floor.

"Tonight, we get some rest. Then tomorrow morning first thing, we take the kid to the rock," Dr. Almasty said. "Dottle! What's for supper? You were so hungry all day. Look in those cupboards and rustle us up some food."

Dottle clenched his fists and glared at the other two. But then he headed into the kitchen and started opening the cupboards.

In Hot Pursuit

Janees Hollow Horn

Racing toward Cullowhee,
North Carolina,
Friday, late afternoon

Our station wagon screamed down the highway faster than I had ever seen it move before. Uncle Jack usually stuck pretty tightly to the speed limit.

"It's not that hard," he said anytime anyone asked him about it. "They print the number on those little white signs every mile or so in case you forget how fast you're supposed to go."

But right now none of us was paying any attention to those little white signs. Chooch was in danger and the bad men who had him were getting away.

We had to catch them. I didn't know what I would

do if they hurt my cousin. It was my fault that they took him in the first place. I would never forgive myself if…

I couldn't bring myself to finish that thought. It really was unthinkable.

I hung my head. I could no longer hold back the tears. Tears of anger. Tears of fear. Tears of sadness.

"Where are you headed, Jack?" Uncle Dynamite asked from the passenger seat. His face was dark and hard. He looked as if he were angry with someone and wanted to grab him by the shoulders and scream in his face.

But he couldn't.

So his face also looked scared. Helpless.

"I'm aiming us at the campus, the last place we know the kidnappers were," Uncle Jack said, his jaw clenched tight. His face was hard, too. But when he turned to look at Uncle Dynamite, I saw a small tear drop from the corner of his eye and slowly slide down his cheek.

That made me cry even harder. Pretty soon I was sobbing. I couldn't catch my breath and gulped for air.

Uncle Dynamite turned in his seat and put his hand on my shoulder.

"It's okay, Wesa," he said in a gentle voice. His face softened a bit and he tried to smile reassuringly. "Don't worry, we'll find him."

"You can't know that," I said between gulps of air. Snot and tears ran down my face like a muddy river.

Uncle Dynamite shifted in his seat, reached into his jeans pocket, and fished out a clean handkerchief. He handed it to me.

I wiped my face and finally got a deep breath.

"It's all my fault," I said.

"No it's not, Wesa," Uncle Jack said without turning around.

"He's right," Uncle Dynamite said. "The men who took Chooch are to blame. You and Chooch did nothing wrong. And as soon as the men took your cousin, you told us everything. I can see why you and Chooch didn't want to tell us the whole truth. But you know your uncle Jack and I believe you. About everything. We will always believe you."

I blew my nose and nodded. Uncle Dynamite knew just what to say to calm me down.

I couldn't believe my uncles just accepted the story about Bigfoot, the Little People, and the glowing rock. I was not even sure I believed it, and I was actually in the story!

Now that my sadness had passed, I was beginning to feel another emotion growing stronger by the minute: white-hot, burning anger.

"Let's get these guys and bring my cousin back home," I said, gritting my teeth.

"Attagirl!" Uncle Jack said.

Uncle Dynamite smiled and patted my knee.

"Once we get to campus, I'm not sure where we'll head next," Uncle Jack said. "We'll have to keep an eye out for that pickup truck."

Then an idea flashed in my mind like the lightning from the magic crystal.

"We can track Chooch!" I said. I smacked my forehead, but not too hard.

"How?" Uncle Dynamite asked. "Did you sneak a bloodhound into the car back at that truck stop?"

"No, Unc. Chooch still has his phone with him. I have him in the Find My Phone app on my phone," I said, pulling my phone out of my back pocket.

Uncle Dynamite looked confused. Uncle Jack said, "How's that?"

"Here—I'll show you," I told them.

I unlocked my phone and launched the app. I clicked on Chooch's phone. A map opened on the screen and I saw a picture of Chooch's phone at a spot at the end of an unnamed road surrounded by green woods. I used my thumb and my index finger to "pinch" the map and make it show more of the area. I could see the college and Judaculla Rock. Chooch's phone was somewhere between the two.

"This is where he is," I said, holding my phone up so Uncle Dynamite could see.

"Jack, he's off Highway 1740 near Tsul'kalu's rock," Uncle Dynamite told his brother.

Uncle Jack sped up even more.

"Hold on, we'll be there in less than twenty minutes," he said.

But I wasn't sure if he was talking to Uncle Dynamite and me or to Chooch.

I squeezed my eyes closed, balled my fists, and thought, "Hold on, Chooch. We're coming for you. Please just hold on."

I repeated this phrase over and over in my mind, like a prayer.

"Hold on. Hold on. Hold on. Chooch, just hold on."

Coming To

Chooch Tenkiller

In a dank basement somewhere, still Friday? Or is it Saturday?

Where the heck am I?

I tried to shake my head, but it hurt too bad.

Blindfolded in a stinky cellar. Angry voices overhead threatening to do something to me.

What did I ever do? I'm just a kid.

Why are these adults so mad at me?

Why did they take me from my family?

What the heck could they want with me?

What?

I thought I heard a familiar voice.

159

Janees?

What do you mean, "Hold on"? Hold on to what, cuz?

No response. I must be hearing things.

Then I heard a terrible scraping sound above me. A long squeak followed and I felt a rush of cool, fresh air. Did someone open a door?

Footsteps.

Then the world grew painfully bright as someone yanked a sack off my head. The person—I couldn't tell if it was a man or a woman—grabbed my sore head roughly and began to pull and tug at the cloth tied around my mouth.

The whole world was spinning. I could make out shapes and colors, but everything was blurry around the edges, like an old picture in my grandma's scrapbook.

The stink of the damp room made my stomach turn cartwheels. I thought I was going to vomit, but I was able to hold everything in. Barely.

As my eyes focused, my stomach settled to a rumbling boil and my heart started to beat faster.

It was the guys who had tried to kidnap me at the college!

"What am I doing here?" I croaked. I didn't realize

how dry my throat was.

The man with the beard and tinted glasses leaned down to look me in the eye. He didn't smile. He just stared.

"You, young man, are going to help us read the treasure map I've been trying to figure out for years," he said. "You're going to help us finally find that hidden Cherokee gold."

I scrunched up my face and slowly shook my aching head.

"Mister, I have no idea what you're talking about. I don't know anything about any map or hidden gold."

"Doctor—it's Doctor," he said.

"What?" I asked, not understanding.

"Not important," he said. The two men standing just behind him shot each other a quick look. "But I know you can read the map. I saw you do it."

"What?" I said again.

"Don't play stupid with me, boy!" he snarled, putting both hands on my shoulders and giving me a painful shake. My world grew dark and then, as he shook me, burst hot white like exploding stars. I closed my eyes tight.

When I opened them, I noticed that the tall man had

pulled out a big knife and held it loosely to his side. For some reason, he was staring at me and smiling, causing the long scar on his face to curve into a C-shape.

I racked my brain in vain for a clue about their treasure map and hidden gold.

"I don't know what map you're talking about. The GPS on my phone?"

"The rock. Judaculla Rock," the bearded man snarled. "The rock is my treasure map and you're going to help us read it."

I closed my eyes and tried to catch my breath. Were these guys crazy? How could a rock be a treasure map?

"Dottle, Nuppence—untie him and take him to the truck. I'll grab my notebook and the other supplies and meet you there," the bearded man said. "Whatever you do, don't let him get away. And for heaven's sake, don't hurt him. Yet."

That last word took my breath away and I almost fainted.

THE TREASURE MAP

Dr. Almasty and His Henchmen

Judaculla Rock,
Saturday morning

Nuppence parked the truck along the road overlooking the big rock. The three men sat quietly as Dr. Almasty raised his binoculars to his eyes and scanned the area for other visitors. He swept the nearby fields—wide open, hilly pastures dotted with cows and ringed by post-and-wire fences. Not a person in sight.

The road to the rock had been abandoned. The truck had passed no other cars. The only other living things—besides the cows—were a handful of buzzards riding the warm wind currents overhead.

When Dr. Almasty was sure they were alone, he grabbed his knapsack off the floor and barked, "I'm heading to the rock. You two grab the boy out of the back and drag him over."

He stopped and looked Nuppence in the eye. "Don't hurt him."

Dottle and Nuppence walked around to the back of the truck. Dottle reached out with his left hand and turned the rusty handle that latched the door. He had to stand on his tiptoes to raise the door all the way. As he stepped back, Nuppence reached in and folded down the tailgate.

The boy was sitting at the far end of the truck's bed with his back against the cab. His hands were tied behind his back. A dirty rag was used as a gag and knotted tightly at the back of his head. Sweat ran down the boy's face. He was shivering even though the morning was sunny and warm.

"C'mon, kid. Get out here," Nuppence said. "Don't make me crawl in there and drag you out by your ponytail. You might get hurt. Bad."

The kid's eyes grew wide and his shoulders tensed. But he used his feet and legs to scoot his bottom across the truck bed. Nuppence and Dottle each grabbed an arm when the boy had scooted close enough and hauled him from the truck, planting his feet solidly on the ground. Dottle reached back and untied his hands. He reached up to untie the gag, but Nuppence shot out a hand and grabbed Dottle's wrist.

"Just one second," he said. He turned to the boy. "One word out of you or if you holler for help, I'll gut you right here and then go back for your family. You hear me?"

The boy shivered, then nodded slowly. Dottle reached up and pulled the gag free.

"Now walk," Nuppence said. The boy looked up at them as if he didn't understand.

Dottle put a hand on his back and gently guided the boy toward the walkway that led to the rock.

"C'mon, now. Let's get this over with, then you can go back to your family," Dottle said in a calm voice.

The boy looked at Dottle over his shoulder with one eyebrow raised in a silent question.

"Psshhhh. Whatever," Nuppence said, pushing the boy so hard he almost fell forward. "Now let's go. You're starting to irritate me."

The boy walked shakily down the path toward Judaculla Rock, where Dr. Almasty stood with his binoculars to his eyes, still scanning the road and nearby fields for approaching trouble. His notebook lay open on the railing above the rock. A stubby pencil looked ready to roll off, but held its position.

"About time, you idiots," Dr. Almasty said. "What took you so long?"

Nuppence and Dottle looked at each other and shrugged. Nuppence used his foot to push Chooch forward toward Dr. Almasty.

"He's here, so stop your whining," Nuppence said. "Let's get to it."

"What? You're giving the orders now?" Dr. Almasty said. "Watch your mouth."

He turned to the boy and smiled. It was a smile like one you might see on a crocodile sliding off a riverbank or on a wolf with its ears laid back and nose crinkled.

"Okay, boy, read me what this rock says while I take notes," Dr. Almasty said. "And no messing around. I saw you reading the rock the other day during your Indian ceremony."

The boy cleared his throat. But then he fell silent.

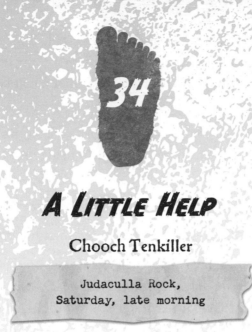

A Little Help

Chooch Tenkiller

How in the world am I going to get out of this mess?

I can't "read" this rock. It isn't a map to some long-lost treasure.

It's a message for all of us. But I couldn't even "read" that message without Uktena's crystal. And that was back in our car, probably somewhere in West Virginia.

With my family.

I really hope they're somewhere safe. Sweat ran down my forehead and into my eyes. I wiped at it with the back of my hand.

I cleared my throat.

"Come on, boy," the bearded man said. "I've waited a long time and you aren't going to deny me my treasure. I've worked long and hard for this. That Cherokee gold is mine."

He nudged my shoulder with the flat of his hand. My head still hurt and the push made my temples throb.

"Cut it out," I said before I could stop myself.

"What did you say?" the bearded man hissed.

"I mean, I can't read the map if you keep pushing me," I said quickly. "I'm hot. I'm sweaty. I have to be in the right mental place to read the rock. Give me a second to get into my trance."

Now I was just making up mystical Indian shaman stuff to stall for time. But only I knew that. The three bad guys seemed to buy it and took a step back to give me some breathing room.

"Siqua hawiya!" I shouted as I raised my arms toward the sky. The bad guys jumped a little, then looked up at the sun and had absolutely no idea I had just shouted, "Hog meat!" in the Cherokee language. "Hadlv saloli?" Yep, I had just asked, "Where is the squirrel?"

Give me a break, I was improvising.

I made my face go blank and lowered my arms. "Agiyosihv!" Okay, that part was true—I am always hungry, which is what I had just said in our language.

The three men looked at me expectantly. I figured I had stalled as long as I could. Now came the moment of truth. Well, my made-up version of the truth. It was worth a try.

I turned to look at Judaculla Rock. The markings in the stone didn't speak. They didn't sing and dance. It was just a big gray rock with old markings scattered across its surface. The man with the beard nudged me again.

"The map is hazy, but I can make out some things," I started. The men leaned in closer. "It says you must travel this road and follow the river through the mountains a great distance. You will travel toward the setting sun, straight as an eagle flies. Then you will find your gold buried under a large hickory tree on a cliff far from here, in what the white man calls Tennessee."

"Baloney," the bearded man blurted out. "The treasure is near here, in these mountains."

"But the map says— -" I started.

"Baloney," the bearded man repeated. "You're lying. You'd better tell us what's really written on this rock or you'll be sorry."

He grabbed me by the front of my shirt and lifted me off the ground. His eyes burned into mine. I had to turn my head because his breath smelled like a wet dog.

My legs started to shake and I started to hyperventilate.

I looked at the other two men in a panic. The short one looked at the ground and shuffled from one foot to the other. But the tall one with the scar sneered at me and ran his index finger across his throat.

The bearded man put me down and poked a finger into my chest. Hard.

"Try again—and no more lies, or so help me, you're a goner."

I gulped. I'd better think of something fast or it could be the end for Chooch Tenkiller. But what could I do?

"Faint," a voice said from behind me.

I turned and saw the Finder standing on the walkway behind us.

"Don't worry, they can't see me," Awatisgi said calmly. "Pretend that the sun and stress are too much and then faint."

I shook my head.

"It'll be okay. They'll take you back to their home," the Finder said. "Don't worry—Tsul'kalu has a plan."

I turned back to the bad guys. I let my face go slack,

wiped my forehead with the back of my hand, rolled my eyes up in my head, and flopped over.

"What now?" the short, round man asked, leaning over me. "The danged kid's fainted. It must be the heat." He actually sounded a little concerned.

The other two men moved closer. One of them kicked me gently in the side. I didn't move or open my eyes.

"Oh, for Pete's sake," the bearded man growled. "Throw him back in the truck. We'll take him back to my cabin, wait until it cools off, and bring him back for another try."

"And this time he'd better read us that map," the tall man said, waving his knife in the air. "Or else it's my turn to ask him some sharp and pointed questions."

Another Task

Tsul'kalu

"I did what you told me," the Finder said, looking up at the giant standing in the middle of his cave. "I went to the Boy at your rock. I told him what you asked me to. But I still don't know why you didn't want me to just grab him and take care of those bad men."

Tsul'kalu nodded. "Yes, I know that you could have done that—you are very brave, Awatisgi. But that isn't what our story tells us will happen."

The rest of the Little People standing around the cave began to murmur.

Tsul'kalu held up his massive hand and the cave grew silent, save for the far-off sound of dripping water.

Light from the fire flickered and made Tsul'kalu seem to move even when he was standing still. The shadow he threw on the back wall of the cave was enormous.

"Our story tells us that the Boy will face several trials before he delivers our message to the world. This is one of them," Tsul'kalu told the Little People. Many in the crowd began to nod their heads.

"But there is one more thing I need for you to do, Awatisgi," the giant said.

The Finder stepped forward. The giant leaned down and whispered into the Finder's ear.

"Yes, I can do that," the Little Person said. "I will go there now."

The rest of the Little People parted to make a path for the Finder as he walked with determination toward the mouth of the cave.

Just before he stepped out of the cave and into the morning sunlight, the Finder turned back to Tsul'kalu.

"I won't let you down," he said, taking off his turban with a sweep of his arm, and bowing from the waist.

"I know you won't," said Tsul'kalu. "I know I can always count on you, my friend."

36

THE OMEN

Dr. Almasty and His Henchmen

Nuppence and Dottle picked up the kid from the walkway and started up the path toward the truck. Dr. Almasty was about fifty yards ahead of them, stomping his feet and waving his arms in the air.

Even though his back was to them, Dottle and Nuppence could make out every word Dr. Almasty was shouting at the trees and surrounding hillsides. None of them was printable.

The two henchmen put the boy in the back of the truck, then closed the tailgate and the door on the cab. They walked around to the passenger side. When he got to the door, Dottle hesitated.

"What?" Nuppence asked with a growl.

"Nothing, I just—" Dottle said, glancing in at the still-fuming Dr. Almasty. "You open it."

"Arggh!" Nuppence said as he yanked the door open. "After you, dummy!"

"Well, get in, you idiots." Dr. Almasty leaned over and said, "We haven't got all day. Let's get the boy back to the cabin and regroup."

Dottle was getting pretty tired of being called dummy and idiot. One of these days, he was going to show both of them! But show them what? Well, he'd certainly show them something. Then they'd be really surprised.

Dottle settled in between the two bigger men. They rode down the hill in silence. Even Dottle kept his thoughts to himself, which was really hard for him. Really, really hard. Dottle just looked down at the floor of the truck and fidgeted every now and then. His stomach, too, was quiet, as if it feared unleashing Dr. Almasty's anger. Again.

Most of the trip back to the cabin was quiet and uneventful. The only excitement came as they neared the hideout, when a large, brown shape rose up from the side of the road in front of them. But rather than running across the road, the creature turned its large horned head toward the truck, blinked its large yellow-orange eyes once, and unfolded two muscular wings. As the three men stared with their mouths open, the great horned owl launched into the sky and circled the truck as it passed.

"What was that?" Nuppence asked. "An eagle?"

Dr. Almasty turned and looked at Nuppence with disdain. "An eagle, Nuppence? Really? An eagle?"

Dottle snorted. Nuppence drove an elbow into Dottle's soft middle, causing the smaller man to gasp loudly.

"Shut up, Dottle," Nuppence and Dr. Almasty said, almost reflexively.

Dottle rubbed his sore ribs and looked down at the floor.

"That owl was a bad omen," he muttered.

"What did you say?" Dr. Almasty asked him through gritted teeth.

"They say an owl is a bad omen," Dottle responded.

"Who? Who says that? Who?" Dr. Almasty shouted.

Dottle and Nuppence laughed.

"What in the blazes is so funny, you idiots?" Dr. Almasty screamed.

Nuppence and Dottle stopped laughing.

"You said, 'Hoo! Hoo!' We thought you were making an owl joke," Nuppence said.

"This is no time for laughter and messing around," Dr. Almasty said as he steered the truck through a gap in the forest and into the long, rutted driveway that led to his cabin. "I've come too far to lose focus now. That treasure is almost mine! And then I'll be able to turn this whole area into one big gold mine."

"Ours," Nuppence said. "The treasure is almost ours."

"Right, right," Dr. Almasty said in a level voice. "Ours. The treasure is almost ours."

The truck rolled to a stop outside the cabin and the three men stepped out into the afternoon heat.

"So what's the plan?" Nuppence asked, shooting a glance back at the rear of the truck.

Dr. Almasty followed Nuppence's gaze. "I've been thinking…there was that other Indian kid with the boy at the college, the one we tried to grab when the boy got away. The one who kicked me. I owe her a smack or two. If the boy can't read the rock, maybe she can."

Nuppence tilted his head and squinted his eyes. "And how in the world do you expect to find her? She and the two old guys are hundreds of miles from here."

Dr. Almasty waved his hand at Nuppence. "Easy. We get the boy to call his family and tell them to meet him at the rock. We'll grab her there and force her to read us the treasure map."

"What about the boy?" Dottle asked, finally catching up with the conversation.

"After he makes the call, we get rid of him," Nuppence said with a grin. "Then we burn this rotten shack to the ground to get rid of the evidence."

Dr. Almasty's face grew red. "Burn this cabin? This cabin that my grandfather built? Burn my cabin? Are you out of your mind, Nuppence?"

As if the worst part of the plan that Nuppence had just outlined was the arson to hide the evidence.

"I just don't want to get caught after we do what we have to do," Nuppence said. "I'm not going back to prison."

"We won't get caught," Dr. Almasty said. "We'll be careful. I have plans for my share of the treasure and they don't involve busting rocks in a striped suit."

Dottle just looked at the two in silence. From the contortions of his face and his intense stare, it was obvious something was troubling him, but neither of the other men asked him what was the matter.

"Dottle, go see if that kid has come to yet and take

him down to the cellar and tie him back up," Dr. Almasty said. "We'll want him to call his family later, so no rough stuff."

Dottle walked around to the back of the truck, opened the hatch and the tailgate, and looked inside. The boy was awake. He again sat with his back against the cab.

"Come on, boy. Let's get you inside and out of this heat," Dottle said in a surprisingly gentle voice. "I'll take you down to the cellar and bring you a cold glass of water, okay?"

The boy just looked at him with a blank expression.

"Okay?" Dottle asked again.

The boy nodded and scooted across the truck bed. Dottle put a hand under his arm and helped him down. The other two men had disappeared into the cabin. Dottle led the boy up the stairs and through the front door.

Dr. Almasty and Nuppence were sitting at the table, drinking big, sweating glasses of sweet tea. Neither looked up when Dottle and the boy walked in.

Dottle gently guided the boy toward the open trapdoor and down the stairs to the dark cellar. Dottle grabbed the flashlight off the short stone wall that stood against the right side of the stairs. He snapped it on and pointed it at the chair in the middle of the room. The faint light coming in through the window high on the opposite wall barely made a difference.

The boy looked up at Dottle. "Do you have to tie me up? I won't try anything. I promise."

Dottle thought for a moment, then said, "I have to tie you to the chair, but I guess I don't have to tie your legs. And I don't see why we need to bother with a gag and blindfold. Just be quiet, okay?"

The boy frowned but nodded at the compromise.

He sat in the chair and put his hands behind his back. Dottle loosely wrapped a rope around the boy two or three times, then tied a simple knot.

"Now shhhhhh," he said. "Those other guys aren't as nice as me. You don't want them to come down here and make you be quiet."

The boy's eyes grew big, but he didn't make a sound. A large bead of sweat trickled down his face.

THE CHASE IS ON

Janees Hollow Horn

Balsam Mountains,
Saturday afternoon

As we sped toward Chooch and the kidnappers, I suddenly shouted to my uncles, "They're moving!"

"What?" Uncle Jack asked without taking his eyes off the road.

Uncle Dynamite leaned back and I held up my phone for him to see.

"Looks like they're headed to the rock, brother," he said. "Head in that direction."

I recognized the road when Uncle Jack turned to speed up the hill, alongside the river. The forests and fields that had seemed so quiet and peaceful a couple of days ago now looked dangerous and foreboding. Even the cows seemed to stare menacingly at us as we drove toward the rock.

Our car rattled and wheezed as Uncle Jack pressed the gas pedal harder than he ever had before. We skidded and slid a couple of times as we rounded curves along the two-lane road.

"We have to be in time!" I said to no one in particular. "We just have to be!"

Uncle Dynamite turned to look at me and tried to smile, but it just looked like he had eaten one too many pieces of corn bread. "We will be, Wesa. Chooch is strong and smart. He'll keep his head and stay safe until we get there."

I hoped my uncle was right. My stomach was flopping like a pair of river otters. The back of my neck tingled. To distract myself, I looked down at my phone. I wanted to see the little picture of Chooch's phone, to feel some sort of connection to my cousin.

Uncle Dynamite and I yelled at the same time.

I saw Chooch's phone on the move again. On the map, it looked like his phone and mine were about to crash into each other.

Uncle Dynamite didn't need to look at my phone to see that.

"There they are!" he shouted as he pointed at the rusty orange truck passing us, heading in the opposite direction. "Get them!"

By the time Uncle Jack found a safe place to turn around in the big old station wagon, we had lost sight of the bad guys.

Well, we'd lost sight of them IRL. But I could see them clearly on my phone.

"It looks like they're headed back to where they were before," I said.

I noticed that Uncle Jack's knuckles were white as he gripped the steering wheel with all his strength. Both of my uncles stared straight ahead. Their faces were pale and I could see sweat running down both of their necks.

I started to cry again, quietly this time.

Uncle Dynamite tapped Uncle Jack on his shoulder and pointed to the highway sign with an arrow indicating right. We turned onto a side road at the sign and sped up another hill. The forest closed in on both sides of us. Even though it was a sunny day, we drove through deep shadows, broken now and then by splotches of sunlight.

"They've stopped!" I said, holding my phone out to Uncle Dynamite again.

This time he took my phone from me, asking, "Okay?"

I nodded.

"Jack, just ahead after the next curve, we're going to turn right," he said. "Keep an eye out for a road or driveway. It might be hard to see."

Uncle Jack slowed the car and all three of us stared out the windows looking for a hidden driveway.

"There!" Uncle Dynamite said.

"Hawa!" Uncle Jack replied. "We're here, Chooch."

We drove up the rutted gravel driveway for what seemed like miles. Then, up ahead, we saw a small clearing and a little cabin. The reddish-orange truck was parked in front.

Uncle Jack pulled over and stopped the car.

"Maybe now is the time to call in the police," he said to Uncle Dynamite.

Uncle Dynamite shook his head quickly. "Tla! They didn't believe us before—called our niece and nephew liars."

Uncle Jack put a hand on his brother's shoulder and gave it a gentle squeeze.

"I know, brother, but we're no match for criminals— two old men and a girl," he said.

"Who are you calling 'old'?" Uncle Dynamite asked. "I prefer Elder-in-Training."

For the first time in a long time, he laughed softly.

Uncle Jack asked, "If we're not going to call the police, what's our plan?"

While my uncles debated our next step, I fished around in Chooch's backpack and pulled out the leather-wrapped bundle. I have no idea why I did that. But I thought if we ever needed the help of a magical crystal, now was the time.

As I unwrapped the crystal, it began to glow so brightly that our whole car was lit up with its blue light. At the same time, it started to vibrate and hum loudly.

"May I?" Uncle Dynamite asked, reaching for the glowing stone.

I handed it to him and all of a sudden, the whole world changed.

"Gado?" Uncle Jack said to himself as he rubbed his eyes.

What we saw was both the most scary and the most exciting thing I had ever seen.

Little People surrounded the cabin three or four people deep. Some Little People sat in nearby trees or crouched on rocks. Some were even standing on the cabin roof, trying to climb the chimney. Most of the

Little People carried weapons of some kind: war clubs, blowguns, bows and arrows. It was a real army ready for war! All they needed was a general to sound the charge!

Then I saw him. Both of my uncles gave soft yells.

"It's him!" Uncle Jack said in an awed voice. "Asduleni. Bigfoot in the flesh."

"That's Tsul'kalu," I said. "He's our friend. He saved Chooch and me from the bad guys once before."

Uncle Dynamite just shook his head as if he couldn't believe his eyes.

Then Tsul'kalu saw us. He motioned for us to join him in the clearing. Without a second's hesitation, we got out of the car and walked over. Uncle Dynamite still held the crystal.

"Ulihelisdi," Tsul'kalu said, raising his large hand in greeting. "Welcome."

"Siyo," both of my uncles said, responding in Cherokee. Tsul'kalu and my uncles talked for a bit in Cherokee. I couldn't follow everything they were saying, but I could understand the basics by watching their body language. Both of my uncles seemed to relax at once. I could see the tension flow out of their necks and shoulders, almost like rainwater running down a rock face.

Tsul'kalu turned to face the Little People who ringed the cabin and said, "Idena! Let's go!"

38

THE FOURTH OPTION

Chooch Tenkiller

In a cabin in the
Balsam Mountains,
Saturday, late afternoon

How did I ever get in this mess? I looked at the dirty floor and tried to pull my hands out of the ropes, but they held. My shoulders and neck cramped.

But this time I wasn't scared or confused. I clenched my jaw and felt my face growing hotter. I shook my head and clenched my fists behind my back. I was angry. These bad guys had no right to take me from my family and try to make me read some imaginary treasure map. No right!

My uncles and cousin must be so scared and worried.

I was going to get out of here and then these

188

kidnappers would be in trouble. I pulled at the ropes again.

Yes! I felt a little give in the loop around my right wrist. I strained again and pulled with all my strength. The knot that held my hands together loosened. I tried one more time and my left hand was free! I was able to free my right hand pretty easily after that.

My arms ached and my hands tingled, like there was electricity flowing through them. I unwound the rest of the ropes that held me to the chair and stood up.

Whoa! Too fast!

I had to grab the back of the chair to keep from falling. I stood there for a moment, just breathing slowly and deeply. I went over my options, trying to make a plan.

1. Go upstairs, push open the trapdoor, and charge the bad guys. Take them by surprise.

2. Wait until the bad guys come downstairs to check on me and overpower them, making my escape.

3. Hide in a dark corner and wait to be rescued.

None of my options seemed realistic. They weren't really options at all. Think, Chooch. What can I do to get out of here?

Just then a fourth option looked in the small window

above my head and waved to get my attention.

The Finder!

The Little Person pulled the window open and leaned his head in.

"Siyo, Chooch. I reckoned you'd figure a way out of your bind," he said.

I stared up at him.

"You coming or not?" he asked with a chuckle.

I dragged the chair over and pulled myself up and out the window.

THE BATTLE

Tsul'kalu

A sound like a thunderclap pierced the room as the double-bolted front door suddenly flew open. A long howl—was it the wind?—followed. The three men inside the cabin jumped up from their chairs at the small table. The tallest one fell backward over his chair as it tipped over.

"What the—?" the bearded man shouted.

The shorter, chubby man ran toward the kitchen, looking for a place to hide, but there wasn't any. He stood with his back to the stove, trembling and wringing his hands.

Then the bearded man stood up straight and glared

191

at the three people standing just inside his door. It was the girl and the two old men! He wasn't sure how they'd found him, but they were playing right into his plans. He'd tie up the old men and drag the girl to the rock and make her read the map. Finally!

"Where's my cousin?" Janees shouted.

"Mind your tongue, girl," the bearded man said, stepping toward her.

"Or what," Janees asked. She hauled her leg back and kicked the bearded man in the shin as hard as she could.

"Why, you little—" the man bellowed. He grabbed at the girl. That's when Uncle Dynamite and Uncle Jack stepped between them and put their hands up.

"Hesdi!" said Uncle Dynamite. "Stop it! Right now. We've come for our nephew and we're not leaving without him."

The tall kidnapper, who had regained his feet, walked around the table toward them. He laughed a cold, hard laugh as he drew a long hunting knife from its sheath.

"What are you going to do—two old men and a kid? You going to overpower us?"

"Yes," said Uncle Jack. "If we have to."

All three kidnappers laughed. They had to hand

it to the three rescuers—they had spunk. But spunk was no match for three hardened criminals in search of hidden treasure.

"Yeah? You and what army?" the bearded man asked with an evil laugh.

Janees brought a leather bundle from behind her back. She peeled back the leather to expose the crystal. When she touched the rock, the three kidnappers jumped. The shorter one yelped in fear.

The cabin was suddenly filled with a horde of Little People pointing weapons at the kidnappers. And there, in the center of the room was Tsul'kalu, whose head brushed the ceiling even though he hunched his shoulders. His large, slanted eyes burned red.

"My army," answered Tsul'kalu in a voice deeper and louder than thunder. "We're here to take the Boy home."

The three kidnappers stared with mouths hanging open. Then the bearded one stepped toward the giant and said, "He's not here."

"Where is he?" Tsul'kalu asked. "He'd better be unharmed."

"He's fine. For now," the bearded kidnapper said. "But you'd better do as I say if you want him to stay that way. If you don't let us go, you'll never find where we have him hidden. He will starve to death and no one will ever see him again."

"No!" Uncle Dynamite said.

"Yes," said the bearded man. "Let us go and we'll call you with his location once we're safely away. Otherwise, he's doomed. And it will be all your fault."

Uncle Jack leaned over and whispered to Uncle Dynamite, "I don't think we have any choice."

"What's that?" the bearded man asked. "You know I'm right. You have no choice except to do what I say."

The three bad guys stood staring at the army, grinning smugly. But their smiles soon turned to looks of shock and dismay as they heard a shout from the open door.

It was the boy! He'd gotten loose!

Dottle sighed with relief, then whimpered.

"What are we waiting for?" Chooch shouted. "Let's get them!"

Janees ran to her cousin and threw her arms around his neck. She kissed his cheek and tears of relief ran freely from her eyes.

Tsul'kalu turned back to his army. "You heard the Boy! Let's get them!"

The shorter kidnapper fainted and flopped over next

to the refrigerator. The tall kidnapper and the one with the beard grabbed and scratched at each other trying to hide under the small table.

Tsul'kalu reached down and pulled each of the two scrapping kidnappers up by the nape of his neck. They swung their arms but couldn't land a blow on the giant. He knocked their heads together once and they stopped struggling. Six Little People grabbed at the short kidnapper's shirt and pants, lifting his limp body off the floor with great effort. They carried him toward the door as the rest of the army followed Tsul'kalu and his prisoners of war outside.

Chooch pulled his uncles and Janees into a giant group hug. They were all crying and trying to talk at once.

Chooch told them what had happened since the kidnapping at the truck stop. The four walked out onto the porch arm in arm. Tsul'kalu and the Little People stood on the edge of the clearing near the station wagon. Propped up against the truck were the three kidnappers, tied tightly with thick ropes. Each had a cloth gag tied around his face.

Uncle Dynamite stepped away from the family. He walked over to Tsul'kalu and handed him the leather bundle.

"This doesn't belong to us," he said. "Wado. Thank

you for bringing it to us when we needed it."

"Hawa," Tsul'kalu said. "This story was written long before we met. I was glad to be here to see it come to pass at last."

With that, Tsul'kalu and the Little People vanished.

"I didn't get a chance to say goodbye," Chooch said, his voice cracking. "I wanted to thank him. There was so much more I wanted to say."

Uncle Jack put an arm around Chooch's shoulder. "He's not gone. He can still hear you. We'll go up to his rock before we leave and put down some more tobacco to thank him properly."

Chooch nodded.

"Well, Jack, now is it time to call the police?" Uncle Dynamite asked, poking his brother in the ribs.

"Oh, yeah, I don't want to take these guys home with us," Uncle Jack said with a laugh. "And we can't very well leave them here for the bears. Poor bears."

Janees embraced Chooch again and held on.

"What's that for?" Chooch said.

"I just can't believe you're really here and safe," she said.

Chooch wriggled out of his cousin's hug, but smiled at her.

"Oh, you'll believe it when we're crammed into the back seat of the car and the farts start."

Everyone laughed. Then all four went into a spontaneous group hug.

"There's nothing stronger than family," Uncle Dynamite said.

"Hawa," said Chooch as he clutched his uncles and cousin tightly to him.

Uncle Jack took out his phone.

"Now what's the number for 9-1-1?"

Chooch and Janees groaned.

THE MESSAGE

Chooch Tenkiller

At the Traveler's Oasis Motel
in Cullowhee, North Carolina,
Sunday afternoon

Pop! Pop!

Flashbulbs were going off all around us as we sat at the long table in the conference center of the motel where we had stayed last night after all the excitement. Microphones on little stands were stacked four deep on the table in front of us. TV cameras stood in a line, pointing at us like some mechanical army. More than a dozen men and women sat in folding chairs in front of us.

The local sheriff had set up a press conference because reporters had been calling him from all over the United States and around the world. He said he even got a call from a reporter in Nepal!

The reporters shouted questions at us, all talking at once. It was all so hard to take.

I looked over at Janees. She smiled and that helped my nerves settle. Uncle Jack and Uncle Dynamite sat in their chairs, fidgeting and pulling at their collars.

Finally, I got up my courage and raised my right hand.

The people grew quiet. I put my hand down and faced the cameras.

"Tell us about your escape."

"What did the men want with you?"

"Did they hurt you?"

"Did your family pay a ransom?"

"How do you feel?"

I raised my hand again. And once again the room grew silent.

"The police have all the information about the kidnappers and their arrest. I'll let them answer those questions," I said. "All I can say about my escape is that my family came for me when I needed them most. And there's nothing stronger than family."

Uncle Dynamite and Uncle Jack both said, "Hawa!"

at the same time. The reporters laughed.

Yes, I left out the part about Tsul'kalu and the Little People. I'm not crazy.

Then, a short man in the back row of reporters raised his hand. He appeared to be American Indian. He was wearing an old-fashioned striped suit and a dark hat, like the bad guys wore in those gangster movies my uncles watched late at night on TV.

"Yes?" I asked him.

"I have a source who said you were able to read the markings on Judaculla Rock. No one else has ever been able to read the rock," he said with just the hint of an accent. "Can you comment on that?"

The room erupted. The noise was so loud it hurt my ears. Reporters' questions came at me like sparks from a bonfire. My uncles and cousin snapped back in their chairs.

I held up my hand again, but this time it took a little longer for the room to quiet.

I looked at the short reporter, who looked sort of familiar, but I couldn't think where I'd seen him before. He looked back at me and tilted his head. "Any comment?"

"Yes, I was able to read the markings on the rock," I started. The reporters all looked at me intently. No one spoke. They were waiting for my story.

My message.

This is what Tsul'kalu was talking about. It was all becoming clear now.

"And?" said the short man. "What did it say?" He smiled and winked at me.

That's when I recognized him! The Finder! Dressed like an old-timey movie gangster. I should have known it was him right away.

I nodded slightly at him and continued my story.

"The markings on Judaculla Rock aren't writing—they're pictures. They represent the smallest creatures among us, the ones that live in our soil and water. They're so small they can be seen only with a microscope."

The reporters started to shout questions again until the Finder cried out, "Hesdi! Let the Boy answer."

The room quieted. I nodded to the Finder again. He looked back at me with a satisfied grin.

"When I looked at the pictures of the creatures on the rock, they began to speak to me. They even sang and danced as I listened to them.

"But their message wasn't a happy one. They told me to warn you—to tell the whole world—that we are heading for disaster. Maybe even the end of the world.

Because our world is fragile. And it's the only world we have.

"When we release chemicals into our air, dump poison into our water, or bury hazardous waste in the ground, we hurt these little creatures. We can't even see them, but we cause them great harm. We hurt not only them, but also all other living creatures.

"Animals are going extinct. Our Earth is warming. Our weather is getting more dangerous. My auntie lost her home to a big storm just last year! We can't drink the water in our rivers. We can't eat the fish. We tell kids they can't play in certain fields or playgrounds."

I paused for a moment. I looked around the room, meeting each reporter's eyes.

"We are hurting the small creatures you see in the pictures on the rock. And they have a message for us."

The reporters all leaned forward in their chairs. Cameras flashed.

"They told me to warn you that what we do to the smallest of creatures, we do to ourselves. If the smallest creatures die, the result will be huge. If they die, we are doomed, too."

The Finder nodded and smiled. Then he was gone.

None of the other reporters noticed.

"They told me to tell you one more thing," I said.

"They said there is still time. There is still time to save them and ourselves. We need to stop polluting the air, water, and soil. And we need to do what they do—sing and dance like in the old days to heal our Earth."

"Nasgi winigalisda!" Uncle Jack said. "Amen!"

Just as the reporters started to shout questions again, the sheriff walked up to the front of the room. He stood in front of our table facing the noisy crowd.

"We need to let Chooch and his family get some rest now. They've been through a lot," he said. "But I will stay and answer your questions about the arrests of a state senator in Raleigh implicated in this kidnapping plot, as well as the suspects who held the boy captive. It seems that the three kidnappers are trying for an insanity defense, claiming that they were captured by Bigfoot and an army of dwarves…"

SAYING GOODBYE

Chooch Tenkiller

At the Traveler's Oasis Motel
in Cullowhee, North Carolina,
Sunday afternoon

We slipped out a side door and caught our breath.

The four of us looked at one another, then we all started laughing. We were all relieved, thankful, and happy to be together.

"I'm proud of you, Chooch," Uncle Dynamite said, putting an arm around my shoulders. If I didn't know better, I'd think he had tears in his eyes. I squeezed him tight, taking in all the scents that reminded me of him: woodsmoke, cedar, and just a hint of Old Spice.

"Me, too, cuz," Janees said. She hugged me again and buried her face in my chest. She grabbed me so hard, she almost knocked Uncle Dynamite and me over. I hope she gets that out of her system before we get back in the car for the long trip home.

"What do you say we hit the road?" Uncle Dynamite said. "We might not make it as far as Chicago tonight, but we can put some miles between us and those bad guys before we stop for the night."

Just then, Uncle Jack's stomach growled loudly.

We all laughed.

"Agiyosihv," Uncle Jack chuckled. "I'm ALWAYS hungry."

We all nodded. Truer words were never spoken.

"I'd really love one of those Carolina barbecue sandwiches before we go," he said, patting his belly. "I've heard so much about them and I haven't had a chance to try one yet. And one thing's for sure..."

"What's that?" I asked him.

"You can't get a Carolina barbecue sandwich in Minnesota," he said, prompting another round of belly laughs.

I hugged him and said, "I still haven't spent any of my souvenir money, so the pulled pork sandwiches are on me!"

We ate at a roadside barbecue stand just down the road from the motel. It was a big trailer painted pink, with a big pink pig snout at one end and a curly pink tail at the other. It was called Meals on Squeals. I'm not kidding.

A line of people waited to place their orders, while families and groups of friends sat at a scattering of picnic tables eating overstuffed pork sandwiches.

Finally, it was our turn and I pulled out my wallet. Both of my uncles put up their hands in protest.

"Please let me pay—I want to," I told them. "Nothing makes me happier than seeing my family enjoying a good meal together. The only thing better would be if I had cooked it. Maybe next time."

Both of my uncles laughed.

After we'd eaten the best sandwiches I'd ever tasted, we walked across the gravel parking lot toward the station wagon.

As my uncles and cousin climbed into the car, I took one more look around me. Cars roared by on the highway. Cars pulled into and out of the parking lot. A solitary buzzard floated lazily overhead, silhouetted against the pale blue sky.

Off in the distance, I saw the bluish-green mountains with their collar of mist that gave the Great Smoky Mountains their name. I could hear the rippling laugh of the river nearby, just out of sight but carrying the lifeblood of this whole area from the mountains to an ocean far, far away. The smell of sweetgrass floated on the breeze, mixing with the smell of barbecue and the flower bushes that dotted Judaculla's hill.

I knew I would miss this place. And I would never be the same after all that my family and I had been through.

And there, across the highway in a grassy field, I saw him.

Tsul'kalu raised his right hand and waved goodbye.

I nodded and then waved back. I gave him a thumbs-up.

Then he was gone.

I climbed into the car and buckled up, ready to start our long journey home.

Acknowledgments

I'd like to thank my friend and agent, Jacqui Lipton, who spends endless hours listening to my many wild book ideas and then helping me focus. I really couldn't do any of this without her. I'd also like to thank my friend and editor on this book and many other projects, Jeff Fuerst, who first heard the germ of this story one sunny summer day three years ago as I stood facing Judaculla Rock and trying to keep a shaky cell phone connection. And finally, I'd like to thank my family, particularly my wife, Laurie, who had to listen to the bits and pieces of this story as I talked them through before sitting down to write. Laurie is now and forever both my muse and my most trusted critic.

About the Author

Art Coulson is a writer of Cherokee, English, and Dutch descent and comes from a family of storytellers. Some of his earliest memories are of listening to stories and reading books on his grandmother's lap. He has been a writer his whole life.

A navy brat, Art traveled the world as a child, attending fourteen schools on three continents before graduating high school. After an award-winning career in journalism spanning twenty-five years, he served as the first executive director of the Wilma Mankiller Foundation in the Cherokee Nation of Oklahoma.

Today, Art lives in Minneapolis, but still visits friends and relatives in the Cherokee Nation several times a year.

About the Illustrator

For more than twenty years, **Frank Buffalo Hyde** has been refining and redefining what is considered to be contemporary Native American art, both as a painter and muralist and as an art writer. He studied at the Institute of American Indian Arts (IAIA) and the Santa Fe Art Institute. His work has been shown in Russia, Japan, France, and at galleries throughout the United States. His paintings are in the Smithsonian's National Museum of the American Indian, the Autry Museum of the American West, and the IAIA Museum of Contemporary Native Arts, to name a few. He currently lives and works in Minnesota.